A CUP OF CHEER

DEB MARLOWE

To Ava Stone and The Pilot
Our Friends Who Are Family

CHAPTER 1

Alexander Nicholas Edgerton, the Earl of Chester, opened his eyes and blinked at the sight of the bosom hovering over him—the delectable bosom that had held him in thrall for these several months.

"Chester, do wake up. You must go."

Still fuzzy from a late night, a quantity of fine, French brandy, and Deliah's not-so-tender ministrations, he heaved a great yawn. But then he grinned and grabbed her. She gave a soft shriek as he bore her down and began to rain kisses over that delectable expanse of flesh.

"Stop now!" She pushed him away. "You will chafe me."

Chester let her go and sat up, running a hand over his jaw. "I thought you said I looked ravishing and rakish with a bit of growth?"

"And so you do. It's fine for when we are alone together at your hunting box, but I wish to wear my blue jaconet muslin today and you know the bodice drops quite low."

"Mmmph." He swung his feet over the side of the bed. All of Deliah's gowns featured noticeably low bodices. It was one of the things that had caught his attention at first, but also one of the things that was beginning to feel . . . predictable.

"It's freezing," he said with a shiver. "Why do we not just lie abed and warm each other up?"

"No. The maid will be in soon. You must not be here when she comes. Go back to your own bed."

He was facing safely away, so he rolled his eyes and mouthed the last words with her.

"Dalliances are one thing. Appearances are another."

Pulling his breeches on, he stood and drained the last of the wine from the bottle on the mantle as he considered the day ahead, the last day of the house party. "Everyone will be setting out tomorrow," he told Deliah. "Would you care to return to London before the Christmas celebrations at the Thorpes?"

"Yes, indeed. In fact, I must go back to Town first, for I've ordered a delightful gown for the Christmas ball." She'd taken up a hand mirror and was making faces into it, searching for lines.

Chester made a mental note to include his finest evening clothes when he packed. He also did some rapid calculations. "We can't stay in Town above three days, if we are to make it to the Thorpe estate in time."

"Mmm," was the only answer she gave.

"Do you think Thorpe will arrange a traditional celebration of the season? Evergreens and wassail and Christmas pudding?" The thought put him in mind of his friend Tensford's cook, who made delightful ginger biscuits. He felt suddenly nostalgic for the Christmas celebrations of his youth. The last few years it had only been drinking and gambling and womanizing—not that different from any other day, to be sure. Pulling his shirt over his head he asked, "What does Knelling plan to do over the holiday?"

He made a face behind the shield of his shirt. But

honestly, it did feel strange to ask his mistress about her husband.

"What do you mean? He'll be at Thorpe's, of course."

His head popped through and he frowned at her. "What do *you* mean?"

She glanced away from her reflection and stared at him, puzzled.

He scowled. "I thought *I* was going to Thorpe's with you?"

She blinked. "Why would you think that?"

"Because we discussed it?"

She waved a hand. "Yes, but that was ages ago and I did not know then that Knelling and his mama would insist on a family Christmas together."

"His mother will be there, too? And now I am not to go? When exactly did you mean to inform me of all of this?"

"Oh, did I not?"

"No," he ground out. "You did not."

"Don't use that sharp tone with me," she warned. "I don't know why you are making a fuss. You'll be busy, in any case, what with the boy to see to."

Chester suddenly found himself longing for the predictability he'd only just disparaged in his thoughts. "What was that?"

"What?"

"Boy?"

"Yes. The boy. You recall. The son of your cousin. The cousin you actually cared for."

"Charles? Charles Edgerton?"

"Is he the one who was gutted by a bayonet in the war?"

His eyes closed. "Yes."

"His boy."

"His boy lives in Suffolk with his tutor, the man's charming wife, his son and one other boarder." He should know. He'd personally searched out the best candidate, a wise fellow of middle age, with a welcoming wife and a son about the same age as Charlie. Chester paid them a goodly sum each month and counted a solid education and a cozy home for the boy as more than a bargain.

"Yes, but he's coming to you for the holiday, or some such."

"How could you possibly know this when I haven't a clue what you speak of?"

"Well, it was in the letter, was it not?"

"What letter?" He was growing alarmed now.

"The one that arrived here just after we did." She gave a huff. "Do not pretend you don't know of it. I distinctly remember discussing it with you . . ." Her words trailed away. "Oh, I did discuss it—with the ladies in the drawing room after dinner that night. Did I forget to mention it to you?"

"It would seem so, madam," he nearly shouted. Crossing to her vanity, he started shuffling through the opened letters stored in a box.

"Keep your voice down," she pleaded. "Don't be cross. I meant to tell you."

Ah. There. He snatched the letter up and started to read through it. "Why in heaven's name are you opening my mail, in any case?"

"It was an accident! I took it from the footman who was searching for you and it got mixed up in my own post." She thrust out a lip. "I didn't think you would mind. It's not as if we have secrets from each other."

"None except for the fact that you are going back to your husband for the holidays?" he snapped. "You swore he cared nothing for you. That he ignores your existence."

"He does, save when it is convenient for him. Or if his mother demands an attempt at reconciliation."

"Reconciliation?" He looked up, aghast.

"Oh, it won't last. It never does," she said casually. "He'll be busy with a new mistress by the time the Season begins and then you and I can meet again."

"The Season?" He stared at her, this woman he'd been prepared to face scandal and ruination for. Hang Society, he'd told her. She could divorce and he would stand by her. He'd lose social standing, risk his honor and connections, but they would be together. She'd reveled in his passionate speeches, but now he began to realize she'd never meant to carry it through.

Had she ever truly cared for him?

Was this truly happening to him, again?

He turned away and focused on the letter once more—and suddenly cursed long and loud. "Damn it, Deliah! Have you ever had a thought for anyone other than yourself? This doesn't say she's sending him back for the holiday, but for good!" He read further. "Hell and damnation! The child is due to arrive in London at noon, today!"

Chester pulled his waistcoat out from under the bed and snatched up his coat. "I must go at once. Damn it, I'll never make it in time."

"What?" Deliah was sitting up straight in the bed now. "You cannot leave today. It is our last today together. We won't see each other for months."

"Have you been listening? A child is about to arrive in London, where there will be no one to meet him!"

"Send a servant, then."

"The boy is my family, my responsibility. Do you know what could happen to him?" he asked furiously.

"We are leaving tomorrow, in any case. Send your valet to fetch him and you can meet them tomorrow evening." She let the sheet fall away and sat back to fully display her assets. "Stay with me, for our last day."

He stared at her. She was lovely. But he was beginning to understand what a colossal fool he had been.

Bending down, he swept up his boots. "Goodbye, Deliah."

~

Miss Julia Deering unwrapped the clutch of carrot tops and laid them on the ground at the edge of the copse. Backing up, she found a spot beneath a tree, cleared it of chestnuts, wrapped her cloak around her and settled down to wait.

It didn't take long for the rabbit to emerge from the undergrowth and start nibbling.

"Eat up," she told him. Raising her head, she drew in a deep breath of cold air. "It smells like snow. If it gets too deep, I won't be able to come out so far—and it will be naught but bark and needles for you, my friend."

The creature, used to her ramblings, ignored her. She leaned back to stare at the sky. She'd have to head home, soon. Lady Chester was napping, but she'd wake before long. Julia, should, perhaps, have stayed inside while her employer was resting. She had plenty to do, between her usual work and the holiday approaching, but she'd been feeling restless. The brisk air and blue sky had called, and she'd come out to tramp the fields and woods and ease her restive spirits. Closing her eyes, she breathed in cold and peace and let the small sounds of nature soothe her.

When she stood, the rabbit didn't startle. It just chewed steadily, watching her. She thought again that it likely wouldn't take much to tame it. She lit up for a moment, aflame with the idea of reenacting Boudicca's act of divination by releasing a hare, but with a sigh, she set out for home. Even Lady Chester might balk at the invocation of Andraste, the pagan goddess of victory, during their Christmas revels.

Moving briskly, Julia left solitude behind and passed through most of the pretty, little village of Farduff. Near the end of the high street, she heard someone call her name. She turned to see Roland Graves hurrying after her.

Curses. She'd nearly made it home to Moreland Cottage, too.

She paused and turned to face the young man. He was grinning, which likely didn't bode well for her. He and the rest of his family, proprietors of the local mercantile, had all been quite distant and disapproving ever since they'd discovered she still ordered fabric and notions from London.

"Good day, Miss Deering," he called as he approached. "We saw you pass, and it appears we have a parcel for your employer."

"A parcel?" She frowned, but did not roll her eyes, as tempted as she was. Since their discovery, Roland and his family had not missed an opportunity to remind her that she was naught but a lady's companion. She eyed him up and down, but he wasn't carrying anything, nor was the boy who trailed behind him. She smiled absently at the child. "I don't recall that Lady Chester has ordered anything."

"Oh, I don't think she's expecting this delivery," he said in a gloating fashion.

"Shall I come back with you to fetch it, then?"

"No need!" Reaching behind him, he took the boy's shoulder and thrust him forward. "Here you are!"

The boy snatched the cap off his head and gave her a very credible bow. He did not speak, however, and his gaze remained fixed on the ground as he twisted the fabric in his hands.

Julia set her jaw and stared at Roland, awaiting an explanation.

"My old auntie came to spend the holidays with us," the man told her, his gaze fastened, as usual, on her bosom. She cleared her throat and he lifted his head. "We're to have a ham and a fine, fat goose, as well."

Roland had also begun reminding her, as often as he could, of the success of his family's business. Sighing, she waited.

"Aunt Williams came through London, where she changed stages at the George. This boy was there, alone. He says he was meant to be picked up by Lord Chester, but no one came for him. The innkeeper sent a servant round to the earl's house, but found it shuttered up, with the knocker off the door. They were puzzling what to do with the boy when Aunt Williams recalled that the Dowager Countess of Chester lives here in Farduff. She brought the boy along with her. They've just arrived."

Julia closed her eyes. She'd heard a great many things about Lady Chester's grandson. Not all of them had been complimentary, but abandoning a child must surely be a new low.

She crouched down so that she could catch the child's eye and sent him a reassuring smile. "Good day to you," she said softly. "I am Miss Deering. What is your name?"

He looked her over carefully. "Charlie Edgerton, Miss."

Julia ignored Roland's snort and mutterings about being presented with a rake's by-blows for Christmas. "Charlie?" she said brightly. "Oh! You must be Charles and Maria's boy."

His hunched little shoulders relaxed a degree. 'Yes."

"You were boarding with your tutor and his family in . . ."

"Suffolk, Miss. But my tutor, Mr. Rule, has . . . left the county."

"Has he? Well, I am delighted that his sojourn has given me a chance to meet you, at last. Lady Chester speaks of your dear Papa, often."

The boy lifted his chin. "He was an officer, killed in the war."

"Yes, I know. I'm terribly sorry. Lady Chester loved him dearly. As a matter of fact, we have one of his uniforms packed away in the attic, complete with pistols and sword, I believe. I daresay you would like to see them."

"Yes, Miss!" He eyed her cautiously. "That is, I don't wish to be any trouble."

"Trouble? To have a boy in the house at Christmas? Lady Chester will count it as luck of the highest magnitude." She raised a brow. "Tell me, do you like Christmas theatricals?"

"Uh, yes?"

"Capital! Then we shall have a grand time." She looked to Roland Graves, who was staring between them with chagrin. "Thank you, Mr. Graves, for delivering Lady Chester's great-grandson safely to us. And please extend our gratitude to your Aunt. I am sure the countess will wish to thank her, somehow."

"I, uh, yes, of course," Roland sputtered.

"Come, Charlie." Julia stretched out a hand. "And tell me, how do you feel about rabbits?"

CHAPTER 2

The sun had sunk below the horizon, and Chester's spirits had fallen even further by the time he rode into the village of Farduff.

He'd missed the boy's arrival at the coaching inn, of course, but the child hadn't been waiting on him when he'd finally got there, hours late. *Taken on*, the staff had said. By an older woman who knew of the family.

What in blazes did that mean? What family? His mother was immured in Devonshire and not likely to set foot beyond the estate. His only other family was his grandmother. Spry as the old girl was, he doubted she'd been lurking in coaching inns, waiting for stray great-grandchildren to come through.

No. The odds were high that the boy had been nabbed by someone unscrupulous. Perhaps they meant to ask for a ransom? Or sell him off into indentured servitude? It could be either of those things or a thousand others in between. Damn Deliah. And damn himself, too, for this debacle was ultimately his own responsibility.

Like so many others.

He'd stared at the porter who had given him the news, feeling empty, save for waves of guilt and remorse. Woodenly, he'd asked for a change of horses and he'd set out for Bow Street and immediately hired the only available Runner. He'd explained the situation, sent the man out to see if he could track the boy—and told him to spread the word amongst his fellows, too.

He would see it set right. He would find the boy if he must hire a fleet of Bow Street Runners or travel himself through the London stews or to the former colonies, for that matter.

But first, he must confess. And he must ask his grandmother to rally her army of connections. No one had a bigger network of acquaintances. Surely, she would spread the word and also know who else he might recruit to help him in the search.

But hell's bells, he'd rather be stretched on the rack.

The temperature was falling as he moved into the village. They had not yet put on their Christmas greenery, he noted. His hired horse slowed as they made their way down the high street. Perhaps the mare sensed his sense of dread . . .

Oh, damnation. No, she'd begun to hobble. The poor beast had gone lame.

Sighing, he dismounted. "Come on, old girl. Home is not far off." He trudged on, leading the mare at a slow walk, watching light begin to glow in the village windows and smelling the savory scents of good, plain, English fare.

"Well, is that ye, my lord?"

Speaking of good, plain English *men*, Chester looked up to see John Simms, the proprietor of the Boar's Head Tavern, lighting the lamp outside his door.

"And weren't the men just speakin' of ye, sir? It's like they conjured ye up with the tattle of their tongues."

He waved a hand. "Good evening to you, Simms."

"Horse gone lame?" The man shook his head. "Bring her around to the stables and I'll have the lads put a poultice on her and give her a nice mash. I'll feed ye up as well. No offense meant, sir, but ye look like ye could use a kidney pie, a kind word and a cup of cheer."

He could, Chester thought. He truly could. It likely wasn't wise to face his grandmother on an empty stomach. He would stop for a meal, a scant few minutes of stolen comfort and perhaps a pint of courage before he went on to Moreland Cottage.

A few minutes later, the mare was being clucked over by a kindly groom and Chester was being clapped on the back and welcomed to the village with uncommon glee. Local men milled about, asking how long it had been since he'd visited, teasing him about his childhood peccadillos, and slyly commenting on his more mature exploits. He bore it until Simms chased them off and made room for him at the bar. Chester thought he saw money changing hands as he sat down and a few last grins tossed his way.

"Here ye are, my lord. Tuck in."

He regarded the plate of hot food and tankard of cool ale with gratitude. Taking a bite of flaky pastry and savory gravy, he closed his eyes in bliss. "Is your sister still minding the kitchen for you, Simms? Or have you gone and found yourself a wife, at last?"

"Wife? Saints, no! I'm far too busy to go courting. In any case, a wife would cut in on my time for experimenting." He set a second, smaller cup down next to the first. "Try a bit o' this, will ye, sir?"

Brows raised, Chester sniffed the amber liquid. "Apple?" Without waiting for an answer, he tossed the drink back.

And promptly coughed, wheezed and sputtered while he wiped his eyes and Simms reached across to pound him on the shoulder. "God's teeth, man! That is strong!"

"But tasty, for all that, ain't it?" Simms asked, full of pride.

"It is, oddly." Chester took a bite of the pie. "But I think I'd best soak it up with dinner."

"Aye, best thing," Simms agreed. "What about you, my lord? You in the petticoat line, these days? Seeing as you have a duty to carry on the line, and all?"

He snorted. "Even a dangling title is not enough to make a good match out of me, Simms."

"What? A fine, braw lad like you? Shoulders like that and an earldom? Ye should be beatin' 'em off with a stick, sir."

Chester took another large bite. His head was starting to spin a little. "Turn it about, to be fair," he said stoutly. "I'm the one who should be beaten with a stick." He suffered a fleeting image of an Amazon beauty standing over him and shook his head. "It's no more than I deserve, and it would likely be less painful than the cuff on the ear and the long-winded lecture, up one side and down the other, that I'm in for."

"Then ye'd better have another, to gird your loins, eh?"

He shouldn't. He knew it. But the tang of apple still lingered on his tongue and the dressing down he so richly deserved loomed ahead. Reaching out, he drained the second cup Simms poured.

He finished his meal, but his head had definitely gone fuzzy. Perhaps it would insulate him from his grandmother's wrath. With an abundance of caution, he managed to put one foot in front of the other and make his way outside—where he stood, blinking and wondering where his mount had gone.

"Oh, yes. Gone lame," he said to . . . no one. He stood alone on the flagstone entrance. Nodding, he set out for Moreland Cottage.

Damnation, had it always been so far? He pressed on, and eventually found the drive, turned and made the long walk to the house. At the bottom of the wide, stately stairs that led to the front door, he paused to catch his breath.

Blinking, he shook his head. Was that *shrieking* he heard, coming from inside the house? Surely not. Just what had Simms brewed into that concoction?

But the noise grew louder, and his alarm kept apace. He could not stand outside in the dark while something nefarious went on in his grandmother's house! He started forward —only to pause when the door opened.

From the lighted portal a shape emerged, screaming. "You'll never defeat the might of Rome, you eye-sore-y woman!" The shadow glanced over its shoulder, then threw itself down the steps.

Before Chester could react, it plowed into him. The figure was small. A child? Nevertheless, Chester was not exactly steady on his feet. He went sprawling backwards with the escapee atop him.

"That's Iceni, you Roman dog!"

Chester and the young person on his chest both looked up. His assailant scrambled away, shouting in glee, clouting him on the head with the stick clutched in his fist as he went. Chester blinked, but the vision above him remained.

It was a goddess, surely. Or the Amazonian figure of retribution he'd conjured up at the Boar's Head. She stood framed in the light, her tall, curving figure outlined in glorious detail. She appeared to be wearing something leafy in her hair and she carried a stick upraised in one hand.

"You shall pay for your heinous crimes," she called.

Chester rose up on his elbows and stared in horror. "I didn't mean it," he said, aghast. "Not truly!"

The vengeful figure lowered her arm. Stepping out, she peered down at him. "Good heavens!" Gripping her skirts aside, she hurried down the stairs. "I am so sorry! Are you hurt?"

He stared up at her. Even in the gloom, he could see her wide, generous mouth and huge, dark eyes shining out from gloriously creamy skin. Surely they could see inside his soul? But her voice was lovely—and full of concern instead of recrimination.

"Sir? Can you speak? Can you tell me your name?"

Chester frowned. His head ached abominably, and there was something moving in his hair and at the back of his neck. Reaching back, he pulled away wet and sticky fingers. Blood?

"Oh, dear." The woman glanced out into the shadows. "Charlie, come back! Run and get Young Robert. I'll need his help to get this gentleman inside. I fear he's addled his wits."

His assailant slunk out of the dark. "I'm sorry, Miss Julia. I didn't mean any harm." The boy peered down at him. He frowned. "Lord Chester? Is that you?"

He didn't want to look away from his avenging goddess, but . . . "Charlie? Charlie Edgerton?" Chester reached up and grabbed the boy by the arm. Real flesh. Not a phantom produced by his drink-and-fall-addled-wits. "Thank God," he said on a gasp.

His hand fell away. He saw the bloody imprint he left on the child's coat. "Oh." He tried to apologize, but his vision was narrowing. He stared at the boy as through a long tunnel —and then everything went black.

JULIA KNEW she wasn't a typical young lady. Not by the standards of the *ton* or even the gentry. She wasn't small and dainty or fascinated by society gossip or the prospect of marriage. She was tall and sturdy and interested in ancient history, colored embroidery threads, animals and old forests. She could dance—rather well, in fact—but she would far rather take a long, brisk walk. Nature, in all of its strange and infinite variety, still puzzled her less than most people.

All the girls her age were focused on flirting and finding a husband. Julia had never met a man who stirred her interest in such a way. No one who had made her swoon or feel flushed and giggly or out of breath—or much of anything at all.

Until now.

This gentleman—he was no ordinary specimen, either. No slim dandy, high, starched collars or spindly shanks enhanced by buckram wadding here. Lord Chester was *big*. Even unconscious and lying prone before her, he emanated masculinity. As she'd cleaned the wound on the back of his head, she'd, for once, felt entirely in sympathy with the tittering maid. She'd had ample time to marvel over the breadth of his shoulders and the musculature of his back. Not to mention how it narrowed down to—

"Well! And so, it is my grandson, after all." Lady Chester entered, the thump of her cane indicating the strength of her emotions. "Is he all right?"

"He has a bump on his head. I believe he got it when he fell back onto the walk. I've cleaned it and put on a bit of sticking plaster."

"And he slept through all of that?" the old woman asked, alarmed. "Should we call for the physician? Drawing near, she leaned down—and then reared back. "Ah. Oh. Passed out with drink, is he? I smell strong spirits." She sniffed. "And apples?"

Julia raised her brow. "I did hear that Mr. Simms has been experimenting with an apple brandy."

The dowager countess shook her head. "Curse the man for getting his hands on Chester before I could." The old lady looked thoughtful. "The boy says Chester knew him, before he blacked out. And that he seemed surprised to find him here."

"He appeared to be *relieved*, ma'am. Perhaps he didn't abandon Charlie as you feared, but merely missed him at the coaching inn?"

"That's giving him the benefit of the doubt."

"It is the holiday season," Julia said lightly. "Goodwill toward men."

"Well, Chester is a good sort." The dowager looked sharply at her. "Despite what the gossips say."

Julia merely nodded. "You would know, of anyone, my lady, that I don't set store by the wagging of tongues."

Lady Chester sighed. "Let him sleep it off. We'll see what he has to say in the morning." She reached out and smoothed a lock of dark hair from his face. "I hope you are correct about the circumstances of his arrival. Perhaps he knows more about the boy's situation, as well."

"Charlie still hasn't confided in you?"

"No. That boy is keeping something close to the chest. Ah, well. We'll see what the earl has to say. Perhaps Charlie will talk to him. And perhaps we can persuade my grandson to stay for Christmas, but I won't hold my breath. He'll likely dash off again, quick as he can."

Julia sternly suppressed the wave of disappointment that washed over her. It was a sign of her contrary nature, that she should finally feel the tingle of attraction—over a pair of shoulders. A lovely, wide pair of—

She cut herself off. It was all nonsense anyway. She'd never gotten on with anyone of his station. Well, except for Lady Chester. But she'd been the first person in society, in her *life*, who viewed her oddities as assets.

Ah, well, as the dowager countess said, he'd probably be gone in a few days. She would keep busy, keep her head down and keep out of his way. He would likely never notice her, in any case.

CHARLIE EDGERTON SANK down into the shadowed corner as the countess thumped by with her cane. He knew it was wrong to eavesdrop, but his straits were dire. He'd let Lady Chester and Miss Julia believe he'd been sent to London for the Christmas holiday. He had not confessed that the Rules had sent him away for good, or indeed, that Mr. Rule had scandalously run off with the curate's wife and Mrs. Rule had gone home to Northumberland in high dudgeon.

He had not wanted the ladies to be immediately focusing on what to do with him or where to send him. He thought he'd give them time to get to know him. Surely, he could be quiet and helpful enough that they would not object to keeping him on?

He only hoped he hadn't ruined his chances, knocking his lordship down like that. But he did enjoy Miss Julia's stories and games, and it had been such a relief to run and yell, he'd quite got carried away.

But then, after they'd carried the earl upstairs . . . he'd started to revise his plan.

His father had admired his lordship. Charlie knew it, because he'd read it in the letters his father had sent home. He'd always reminded his mother to take any troubles to his cousin, as Lord Chester was a true friend. And Charlie had liked the man himself, the few times he'd met him. He knew the earl had taken great care in choosing Mr. Rule as his tutor. Charlie had been happy there—until Mr. Rule had broken his word, and his vows.

That was the thing. Charlie's father had written that Lord

Chester always kept his word. So . . . if Charlie could get him to agree to let him stay . . .

Except—his lordship was wild. He'd heard Mrs. Rule whisper it. He'd heard it again at the George, during those long, frightening hours when he'd waited for someone to come for him. Lord Chester was always away from home, chasing skirts, they'd said.

Well, perhaps he would stay at home if he had a wife? Perhaps he would enjoy chasing Miss Deering's skirts? He wondered what the earl would do with her skirts when he caught them, but he thought it safer not to ask. But Charlie found the lady's companion to be a right one, sure enough. Why wouldn't the earl?

And why wouldn't they wish a boy to help them make a home?

He slunk back to his room, thinking hard. It might be better if he found a way to hurry their courtship along. If his great-grandmother was right, they only had a few days. Was that enough for the two of them to fall in love?

He knew just who to ask. His new friend Nick seemed to know everything. He'd known how a kind word would help while Charlie stood in the mercantile today and listened to the Graves family make vulgar assumptions about him. Nick had promised to show him the secret meadows where the deer gathered to play. And he'd told him just when to go out tonight, in time to see a shooting star streaking across the sky. Charlie had done as he'd said, and sure enough, he'd seen the largest, longest shooting star imaginable.

Surely Nick would know the secrets of courtship, as well.

He would ask him tomorrow.

CHAPTER 3

Chester woke with a pounding head, a foul taste in his mouth and the utter certainty that he'd never eat an apple again—and that would be no small feat here at Moreland, renowned for its orchards. Groaning, he managed to ring for a servant, then he sat at the edge of the bed, his head in his hands, until the man arrived. He ordered a hot bath and a pot of hot coffee and partook of them together.

Afterward, he felt nearly human again, so he ordered tea and a rack of toast. And after that, he knew he could not delay any longer, and he went off like a man, to take his medicine.

As it was not quite noon, he knew he'd find his grandmother in her rooms, seeing to her vast correspondence. He poked his head in and she glanced up, raised her brows, set down her quill and beckoned him in.

"Survived the night, did you?" she asked wryly. "I should think you'd know better than to sample one of Simms's concoctions."

"I did know better, but I thought I was coming here to

make a terrible confession. I let my utter dread affect my better judgement." He sank down into a chair with a wince.

"Make all the faces you care to, you'll get no sympathy from me," she told him. "A sore head is nothing next to the trials of growing old."

"I well believe it." He shot her a fond glance. "But I am grateful that you suffer, as the alternative does not bear thinking of."

"Hmmph." She looked pleased at his words, though. Unfortunately, it didn't last. "Terrible confession, eh?" she repeated in sharp tones. "I take it you *didn't* know that Charlie was here, then?"

"No," he sighed. "Indeed, I was coming to let you beat me for missing him at the coaching inn and to beg you to rally your network of spies." He nodded toward her stack of letters. "And then I was going to hightail it back to Bow Street and continue to hire every available runner."

"Well, I give you credit for wise planning, but it was damned careless of you to leave the boy in such a situation."

"I know. And although I hadn't an inkling of his arrival in London before yesterday morning, I know it's no excuse. I was responsible for the circumstances in which the news went astray." He leaned his head back. "I have no notion how he arrived here, but I am truly, deeply grateful." He shuddered. "The scenarios I imagined . . ."

"Do not share them. I've conjured enough of my own." She explained how the boy had ended up at Moreland Cottage.

"Well, thank God for Aunt Williams. I shall buy her a fur. How old is she? Perhaps a tiara." He laid his head against the high back of the chair again. "When I woke this morning, I thought I might have dreamed the boy." He rubbed his temple. "I'm afraid I have only the most bizarre recollections of my own arrival. Screaming. And blood. And a Valkyrie with a stick for a sword."

"The blood was your own," his grandmother said with a nod toward his head. "The noise was Charlie, I'm given to understand. And that was no Valkyrie, but my companion, Miss Deering."

He frowned. "You've hired a companion?"

"Yes, and so you would know, had you deigned to visit me over these last two years."

That blow hurt worse than his head, weighted as it was with the truth. He pressed his lips together. "You are right. I am sorry."

Closing his eyes, he allowed the silence to stretch out for several moments. "I'm tired, Grandmama. Worse, I think I've . . . wandered off course. I don't know where I'm going, any longer."

When he opened his eyes, he saw her expression had softened. "Would you mind if I stay for Christmas?" he asked. "I admit, I've been having a nostalgic fit for carols and greenery and figgy pudding and all the rest."

"And a cup of cheer?" she asked with a grin.

He shuddered. "Perhaps not for a day or two." Sighing, he let his thoughts wander back. "It would be nice if we could have a holiday like we used to, before . . ."

"Well, you know I'd like nothing better than to have you stay with us, but I must warn you, Christmas has been rather quiet in this house the last years."

Chester straightened. Perhaps the coffee was taking effect at last, as his head didn't feel as if it might roll off. "Well, we must do something about that. We have a boy in the house, this year."

She waved a hand. "I'm too old for all of that effort, now."

"Your companion could manage it, I should imagine."

"Miss Deering is a treasure. I attend to my correspondence and she keeps everything else here running in tip-top shape. She's an organized wonder. She has a golden touch, dealing with touchy modistes, obstinate grocers or tradesmen of any sort. Well, except for the Graves family, here in the village, but I swear, they are impossible."

"Roland Graves," Chester said, making a face. "He was always a weasel."

"Nor has he improved with age. In any case, Miss Deering has exquisite taste and a good heart. But the poor girl appears to have no familiarity at all with the trappings of any holiday. I don't think she knows anything about a traditional Christmas, and I don't believe she's ever truly had a happy Christmas, herself."

"Oh? That sounds unusual."

"No mother," his grandmother said bluntly. "Her mother died giving birth to her and she's had no real female influences. Her father was a scholar. A brilliant man, but not aware of much beyond the confines of his desk, I gather."

"Hmmm." Chester considered the problem. "Well, I have plenty of fine memories of happy holidays. I can help. It shouldn't be too onerous. We must give Charlie some merry memories to take on with him, when I've found him a new place."

"A new place?" she asked sharply.

"Yes. The letter I finally received yesterday said that Mr. Rule was no longer going to be tutoring. I shall have to find the lad a new situation."

"So. Perhaps that is what has been bothering him. I could tell something was eating at him." She looked down at her letter. "Yes. I like the idea more, as I think on it. The magic of Christmas. Let us have a holiday full of the sounds and scents and tastes of the season."

"It's decided, then." Chester stood and crossed behind her

desk to bow over her hand. "Thank you, Grandmama. You have ever been a port in the storm."

Her mouth twisted. "Yes, well, perhaps you might think of sailing in calmer waters."

He snorted.

"And Chester?"

He paused.

"You are to be nothing but kind to Miss Deering. *Nothing but*. Do you understand?"

"I'm hurt you felt you needed to ask." A heavy sigh escaped him. "I need a rest, Grandmama. A time to think. I'm not about to chase after your companion." Though she might have the prettiest, kindest brown eyes he'd ever seen. Or had he dreamed that?

"Good. I care for the girl. But the person I care most for in the world, is you."

She squeezed his hand before she sent him off and he went out, feeling better than he had in some time.

"I'M THRILLED beyond measure to have your help with my piece," Julia told young Charlie. "I've always wished to write a dialogue between Boudicca and a Roman nemesis." She held up the *papier mache* helmet they'd fashioned for him and contemplated how to manage a red crest. "But your contribution to the theatrical should not also be about her story. You must choose something that excites *you*."

"But I don't know what to choose," Charlie answered, worrying his lip.

"Can you think of something that you enjoyed studying with Mr. Rule? It could be anything. We could even make mathematics work, if that is your passion." Although, very privately, she thought such a choice would be dull—and probably beyond their small audience.

Charlie made a face at the suggestion, however. Thank goodness.

"What was your favorite thing that Mr. Rule taught you?"

He frowned. "Well, one time we did recite Reverend Warton's *The Grave of King Arthur*. I quite liked that one, with the great hall and the bards in the gallery and the golden cups—but especially the tale of how the elvin queen saved King Arthur after he fell. She healed him with dew and magic and took him to her faery isle, until he would be needed again."

Julia's heart softened and she wondered if the boy had imagined such a fate for his own father, fallen in battle. "That sounds grand. Perfect, in fact." She set down the helmet. "We can make you a crown to wear. And a tunic, with a dragon rampant." She grinned at him. "Your piece will be the most exciting of the day!"

"Do you think so?" The boy's face lit up with enthusiasm, but even as she watched, she saw him try to rein it in. "If it is not too much trouble?"

"Not at all. We shall do it together and have a grand time of it."

They sketched out some ideas and Charlie seemed to relax. Lady Chester was right. The boy carried the weight of something, but he looked happy as they made plans. As they wound down, however, his smile faded. She kept quiet as she put her colors away, waiting to see if he would speak of what troubled him.

"Can you cook, Miss Deering?" he suddenly blurted out.

"Cook? Me?"

He nodded and appeared to be anxiously awaiting her answer.

"Well, a little, I suppose. The cook in my father's house

did show me how to coddle eggs and make bread. But not much beyond that. Why do you ask?" A thought struck her. "Is there a special dish that you might like us to ask Mrs. Jensen to prepare? One that you associate with the coming of Christmas?"

"Well, that wasn't why I asked . . ." he hedged.

"Why, then?"

He shrugged. "It's just something my friend Nick said."

"Nick? Is he a boy from the village?"

"He's not a boy. He's older. Not as old as Lady Chester, though, I don't think. He lives north of the village, he says. He's just . . . nice to be around. He knows so many things. This morning he showed me how to get past the thorns to the last of the winter berries, tucked deep in the center of the bush and protected from the frost. I asked him if he was married and he said he was. So, I asked him how a gentleman knows the right lady to marry."

"What was his answer?" And why was Charlie thinking of such a thing?

"He just patted his middle and told me his wife says that the way to a man's heart is through his stomach." He gave her a sidelong glance. "But now that you mention it, I do remember my mother's Christmas pies," he said a little wistfully. "Do you think cook would teach you . . . us . . . to make them?"

"I'm not sure." Julia had never given thought to interfering in Mrs. Jensen's domain. She wasn't sure the cook would welcome such a suggestion. "Do you mean the kind of pies with minced meat and fruit?" she asked cautiously.

"Yes," he agreed with enthusiasm. "My mother always made them shaped like little mangers, just like where the baby Jesus was laid."

"Ah, well—"

"Did someone mention Christmas pies?"

Charlie spun around, his eyes wide. Julia rose to her feet and dropped a curtsy. "Lord Chester. Good afternoon. I do hope your wound is healing." She stood there, trying to maintain her dignity while all of her nerves went aflutter. Goodness. She'd thought he was big when he was lying prone before her. Now he seemed . . . monumental. She was tall for a female and she'd never met a man who towered over her in such a way. Both she and the butterflies careening inside her appreciated the novelty of it.

"Oh! Yes?" Frowning, he touched the back of his head. "Yes. Thank you. I'd nearly forgotten it."

Charlie bowed. "I am glad to hear it, my lord. I offer my apologies."

"No, no. There's no need for you to apologize, lad. It was my own fault entirely. I should have moved out of your way. I blame my own bad judgement." His mouth twisted. "As well as my surprise at finding a Roman dog escaping the confines of Morland Cottage." Laughing, he bent down and grinned at the boy, clasping his shoulder. "Think no more of it." Growing more serious, he addressed Charlie directly. "I offer my own apology for missing you at the inn yesterday. It was very badly done of me."

Watching, Julia surreptitiously gripped the chair she'd been sitting in. Lord Chester's hand looked huge against Charlie's thin shoulder. The man possessed physical strength and societal power. Truthfully, the thought of him here frightened her. He seemed to embody all the elements that had always worked against her.

And yet . . . to see him treat the boy with just the right amount of fellowship, to hear him offer an apology of his own . . . it was so far beyond her experience with gentlemen of his class, it seemed a miracle of the season.

"No worries, sir." The boy beamed. "It all worked out fine."

"Thank the heavens, it did." The earl stood. "I'm thankful that you are safely here."

He'd found a new shirt somewhere, Julia noted, as she knew the maid, Susan, had the bloodstained one from last night soaking in the laundry. He wore fawn colored trousers and a loosely cut, blue coat that made his eyes shine like sapphires. No wonder he had a reputation with the ladies. She could scarcely look away.

"Now." The earl rubbed his hands together. "What was that about Christmas pies?"

She cleared her throat. "Charlie mentioned that he recalls his mother's pies fondly, my lord."

"Please. You both must call me Chester. All of my friends do." He nodded. "There's no need to be formal, as the three of us will be working closely the next few days."

"Sir?" Nerves of a different sort jumped inside of her.

"It's true. I spent some time with my grandmother this morning. Her ladyship has spoken. She's issued her decree and charged us with a solemn duty."

"What duty?" Charlie asked, his eyes wide.

"We are to usher in a grand Christmas to the house, this year. A jolly holiday with all of the senses engaged. Every tradition observed."

"Traditions?" Julia's awe gave way to anxiety. Christmas traditions? She was woefully unprepared for such a task. Church services and a roast duck when her father remembered to order one had been the extent of her childhood observances.

"Yes, and I've just spoken to Mrs. Jensen. She is prepared to do her part. Charlie, you'll be glad to know that she usually does serve a Christmas pie, most often after dinner on Christmas Eve. She has a grand feast prepared for Christmas day, and the plum pudding has been underway for weeks."

"That does sound wonderful," Charlie mused. "But surely there must be something Miss Deering can make."

"We do have something of an original tradition here, sir," Julia rushed in. "For the last couple of years, we've put on a Christmas theatrical as a treat for the servants and their families. We've done it on Christmas evening, sort of an ushering in of Boxing Day, when they rest from their labors."

"A theatrical?" He raised a brow. "Individual performances? Or a play?"

"Individual pieces. Charlie and I were just working on ours."

"And does my grandmother take part?"

"She does. She's done something from Wollstonecraft twice now."

"Of course, she has," he said. "My grandmother's feelings about the rights and abilities of women are well known." But there was a frown hovering at his brow.

"She swears she's got something different planned for this year, though she's being quite secretive about it."

"I find myself torn between avid curiosity and dread," he said with a shiver.

"You must perform with us, as well, sir," Charlie said.

Lord Chester laughed again. "I'm afraid none of the poetry I know is fit for polite company."

He glanced over at her and Julia's breath caught. No one had ever shared such a conspiratorial, slightly devilish look with her.

"Will you learn something, my lord?" Charlie asked eagerly.

"I will, lad. If you will call me Chester."

"Yes, sir. I will. I mean, I will, Chester." Frowning, the boy gazed intently at Julia. "But still, there must be something . . ."

He walked over to the window and gazed out. The earl raised a questioning brow, but she could only shrug. Then

Charlie spun around. "I know!" He was triumphant. "Chestnuts. Surely you can roast chestnuts, Miss Deering? We used to buy them from the street vendors in the winter, but my father did mention that he used to gather and roast them with you, uh, Chester?"

Lord Chester nodded. "Yes. We did, indeed."

"Then you must enjoy them? I know I do. Miss Deering, can you roast chestnuts?"

"Well, of course. That is, I can certainly try."

"It does sound like a good beginning to our project," the earl agreed. "I'm reasonably sure I can recall where we used to collect them. We can troop outside in the fresh air and make plans for our project as we go, then come back and warm ourselves by the fire."

The warmest smile bloomed on Charlie's face, the truest one she'd yet seen from him. "Yes, let's go, shall we, Miss Deering?"

What she should do is stay behind and allow the two of them to go out together. Surely the boy could use some time with his family, and she could use a chance to discipline her reactions to Lord Chester. "I should check with the countess, to be sure she doesn't need me," she hedged.

The boy's smile began to fade. She sighed. "But if she does not, then yes, of course, we should go. We can bring back enough to share with the dowager and the servants." Julia nodded at the boy. "A good idea, Charlie. Why don't you run and fetch your coat and hat?"

"Will you need to change, Miss Deering?" the earl asked solicitously.

The measuring look he gave her sent a shiver down her spine. "No, sir. It shouldn't take me long." She gave him a nod and hurried out, feeling unsettled by the weight of his gaze on her as she went.

CHAPTER 4

Chester breathed deep and let the cold air chase away the last remnants of his headache. The day shone clear, the air burned crisp—and he was a damned lucky man. Charlie raced ahead as they ventured beyond the village to the wooded outskirts. The boy kicked up dead leaves and laughed as he blew great clouds of warm breath and Chester sent fervent thanks toward the heavens. The boy was safe. They were together—what remained of their small family— at least, those who wished to be a part of it. And he found himself relieved to be out of the usual, madcap social whirl of his life.

He drew in the scent of the woods. This was what he needed. Family. Peace. Christmas. Time apart, to contemplate.

There was only one distraction from this contentment— and he eyed her warily as he wondered what to make of Miss Julia Deering.

Granted, she definitely caught his eye. She was tall—a point in her favor. He liked a woman he did not have to peer down at. Though they were not flamboyant, she had curves.

And style. The warm looking, woolen day gown she wore complimented her figure—but also featured a lighter blue ruffle that framed her face and drew attention there. And the cloak she had come downstairs in . . .

"Your cloak is stunning, Miss Deering. That embroidery catches the eye so that one can scarce look away."

She looked gratified. "Thank you. I did the work myself. I am happy with how it turned out."

He was impressed, despite himself. The white and silver decoration, done up in Celtic symbols, ran down the front and along the hem of the garment. "Was it your own design?"

"Well, of a sort." She gave a sheepish shrug. "It goes along with my latest fascination—the Picts and Celts and the story of Boudicca. I'm doing my theatrical piece on her this year, as a matter of fact."

"Ah, yes. The theatrical." The idea only added to his . . . worry. Clearly, another of his mistakes—not keeping in touch enough to know that his grandmother had hired this girl and made her part of the household. Who was she, really? Pretty brown eyes, aside, the little his grandmother had said about her had not felt promising. She'd had no experience of a happy Christmas. No comprehension either, if she thought Wollstonecraft and Boudicca to be fare for a holiday program.

All that was understandable, given the circumstances his grandmother had mentioned, but what of life's other pleasures? Did she lift the countess's spirits? He sincerely hoped she did not turn out to be dour and joyless. His grandmother did not need another like that in her life. Nor did he. His own mother filled that role with enthusiasm, already. "How did that come about?"

"The theatrical? Well, it was my idea, actually. Lady Chester was kind enough to indulge me—and to take part."

"It's an unusual notion—at least, to include it around the holidays."

"Is it?" She looked startled. "There was a family, near our home outside Oxford. They had four daughters. The girls always did a Christmas theatrical each year." She gave a little laugh. "I thought it was another, usual part of the holiday."

"Perhaps. Did they keep their performances related to the Christmas season? Hymns? Caroling? A nativity?"

"I doubt they did a nativity, as our church services usually included one. But I don't really know."

"Why not?"

She gave a shrug and stepped around a log fallen across the trail they followed.

"Did you not attend the theatricals?"

She flushed. "No."

He stopped, staring down at her from atop the log. "Ah. So you wanted to recreate what you missed as a child?"

"Yes." She raised her chin. "I suppose that sounds foolish to you?"

"Not at all. In fact, I approve, wholeheartedly. How could I not, when I've spent so many years chasing that which was denied me in my own childhood?" He hopped down and started forward again, calling out to Charlie. "Yes, lad. That's the one!" The boy was circling the tree where he and Charles used to gather chestnuts.

Disappointment showed on the boy's face as he drew closer. He stared upwards. "None left on the ground, sir. And only a few, very high up, on the branch."

"Ah. I suppose the villagers have been here before us."

"I can climb up," Charlie offered.

"Hardly worth the risk. Even the squirrels must have had difficulty getting those."

The boy looked like he might insist, but Miss Deering stepped forward. "No need. I know a place where there are still plenty to be found." She looked askance at Chester. "It is rather a long walk, though. If you prefer to return to the cottage, I will take Charlie onward."

"Do I look so faint-hearted to you, Miss Deering?"

She colored again. "No, sir. I just thought your head might be aching."

"It is not, thank you. But if it were, I could not now admit it, not for all the letters in grandmother's desk."

That made her laugh—and Chester felt an uncommon thrill. She lit up when she smiled, her dark eyes flashing and her whole face wreathed in good humor. It gave him a bit of hope. Perhaps she was not dour and joyless, after all. With a smile like that, he would enjoy proving himself wrong. "Lead on, Miss Deering. We are at your disposal."

HER NERVES finally began to settle as they moved on. Out here the earl's presence did not seem so overwhelming. He kept his distance and his manners were fine enough, although she felt as if he were still measuring her. Fair enough, as she was doing the same to him, although she was relieved he did not act the least like his reputation might suggest.

She focused her attention on Charlie as they walked, showing him the protected little hollow where an old log still sprouted with a forest of toadstools and later an oak with a staircase of shelf fungi marching up the trunk. When she stopped to point out a raven watching them from high in a tree, Lord Chester stepped closer.

"You know, it's been a long time since I walked the countryside instead of riding through."

She sidled away. "Yes. I know it's not fashionable to walk, but I've no means to ride." She steeled her spine, bracing herself. At least he'd waited until they were away from the house before he began to remark upon her deficits in the ways of a young lady.

"It's perhaps a benefit, at least out here. You forget how much there is to miss, going by too quickly."

She gave him a quick, shocked look, then glanced away.

"You must be a prodigious walker, Miss Deering. You seem very familiar with this route."

"The early British people lived their lives much more connected to nature. I like to walk and think about how that must have been." She shrugged. "Mostly, I just like to walk." Deliberately, she ignored the tawny highlights the sun brought out of his chestnut hair. "Especially out this far, where nature is busy, but still, there is a peace to be found that one cannot experience in the village."

"True enough." They all fell silent then, as she led the way onward, but to her surprise, it was a comfortable, companionable sort of quiet.

She paused when they drew near the spot. "Would you mind hanging back a moment?" she asked the earl. "While I show Charlie something?"

He made a motion for her to proceed. Kneeling down, she looked solemnly at the boy. "Do you recall what I told you about my little friend?"

He looked eagerly about. "Yes! Is this the place?"

"Can you step quietly and stay behind me for a bit?"

He nodded and she moved quietly ahead, stopping near the brush where the rabbit's warren was located. She pulled a bag from her cloak and gave a soft whistle.

After a moment, a small black nose poked from the underbrush. It wiggled and then the rabbit inched out.

Charlie's breathing quickened with excitement. Julia knelt and pulled a few cabbage leaves from her bag. Moving slowly, she stepped forward and spread them on the ground before backing up to where the boy waited. The rabbit was chewing industriously before she made it.

"He truly does know you," Charlie whispered.

"Yes. We've become friends. Since the cold set in and foraging has become difficult, I've begun to bring him scraps."

"Can I touch him? Hold him? I'm sure I could scoop him up before he got away!"

"You likely could. I know it's tempting, because I had the same thought. Let us think about it, first? Imagine how he would feel. Caught? Trapped? Terrified? Why not let him get to know you instead? Learn your scent. Your ways. It's much better to let him grow to trust you, don't you think?"

The boy agreed, but did let out a sigh and he watched avidly as the rabbit nibbled away.

"Why don't we gather our chestnuts?" Julia asked after a few moments. "If we move slowly and try not to be loud, he might stay to watch us."

"Where?"

She pointed beyond the brush, toward the copse of trees, where chestnuts littered the ground and still hung from branches.

They began to collect them, peeling away the prickly hulls from those that needed it. As the bag began to fill, the earl moved to join them. Charlie's attention was torn between their task and the rabbit. The little creature finished the cabbage, but continued to nibble on bits of grass and bark as they worked.

"It's going back in," the boy called at last.

"And our bag is filled," Lord Chester said, hefting it high. "Let's head home and share our spoils, eh?"

Charlie stayed a moment, creeping close to the under-brush to see if he could spot the entrance to the warren and the earl stepped close to Julia.

She stared up into the bold features of his face. He was so unlike the aristocrats she'd known. He was large and utterly masculine, as if he was not *quite* civilized. And to her dismay, something inside of her liked that hint of virility, the smolder of something perhaps dark—but in no way boorish—that he carried around with him.

Her reaction was troubling. His mere presence agitated her. When he moved close, she felt the turmoil growing inside of her.

"You have a soft spot for animals, Miss Deering."

"Yes, I suppose I do."

"I have learned to have a fondness for them myself. It's so much simpler to love an animal, is it not?"

"A thousand times easier," she agreed vehemently. "Animals act on circumstance and instinct, without artifice or judgement."

"That was a valuable lesson you gave Charlie," he murmured. "And well-taught." He leaned in and her heart jumped. "I'm afraid every boy's first instinct is not always to let other creatures live in peace." With a nod, he moved away and beckoned Charlie. "Come, let's have a song as we head back! Shall I sing for my theatrical debut?"

The boy came running and they walked ahead, belting out a Christmas carol. She stared after them a moment.

Oh, no. No, no, no.

She would not be so foolish.

And yet, her step was light as she set off after them and she hummed a bit of the song as she went.

"THERE IS A TRICK TO ROASTING CHESTNUTS," Chester said. They all three sat before the fire, with all the necessary tools spread out around them. After so long in the brisk air, the warmth felt like a welcome.

"Be careful of your fingers, lad," he said as he passed the boy a small knife. He extended another toward Miss Deering, careful not to brush her fingers.

He was feeling a bit better about his grandmother's companion. She had taught Charlie an important lesson and done it with natural ease and without judgement. In truth, it had eased some of the anxiety he felt about her, but not all of it. Much as he hated to admit it, his grandmother was aging. He still wished to see how the young lady acted around her, and what role she filled in the house.

And belatedly, he realized he would have done better to bring along a chaperone other than Charlie on their outing today. If he suspected the girl might be an opportunist taking advantage of his grandmother, there was nothing to say she might not do the same to him.

Of course, she seemed to be just as wary of him as he was of her—and that just might be the best sign of her innocence and good judgement.

She watched him now with quiet attention that could not quite cover that guardedness. She gave a small, quick smile of thanks, though, and he found himself struck again by the brightness of her dark eyes. Lovely eyes, really, large in the slender angles of her face—

"What is the trick, sir?" asked Charlie.

Chester blinked. "Well, as they've all been wiped clean, now we must make a slice through the outer shell. If you do not, the pressure builds inside and it will explode, once it heats up."

"Oh! Is that why the street vendors carve an X into the end of it?" She proceeded to make the mark on one of the chestnuts.

"It is. You must make your slice go deep," he cautioned.

He turned to Charlie. "Your father and I preferred to slice along one long side, like so." He demonstrated for the boy. "As it roasts, it opens up like a clam."

"Like this?"

"Yes. Careful. Make your cut a little deeper. There. Perfect. Now, into the pan and let's do the rest."

"I prefer the X. It reminds me of home." Miss Deering proceeded to make quick work of several more chestnuts.

"As you like, as long as you go through the shell."

They were quickly done, with the three of them working, and he set the pan over the coals. "Now, we wait."

Climbing to his feet, he assisted Miss Deering as well, and saw her settled in a chair pulled close to the fire. He took the other chair while Charlie lounged at their feet. "So, shall we discuss our plans for other Christmas festivities?"

Her eagerness deflated a bit. "What did you have in mind?"

"What would you like?" He watched her closely. "What makes you think of Christmas?"

She thought about it a moment. "Greenery, spread throughout the house. I've always . . . that is, I believe everyone would enjoy that."

"Well, that is a given," he declared. "In fact, I was watching closely today, as you led us so far afield, and I noted several spots that will yield us enough holly, laurel and fir."

"The fir trees always make me sneeze when I get too close," she said with a grin. "But I imagine the smell will be lovely."

"Can we go out tomorrow to fetch it back?" Charlie asked.

"Alas, Mrs. Eckles will not have it in the house before Christmas Eve," Chester told him. "The housekeeper has always believed it's unlucky to bring it in any earlier, but yes, we can go out and collect it tomorrow. We'll store it in the tack room in the stables and perhaps Miss Deering might help us weave a few garlands, if we ask her politely."

"Yes, please?" Charlie turned to her in excitement. "And red bows? Can we have them? My mother always had red bows tied in the greenery."

"Then we must, as well," the young lady assured him. She leaned down toward him. "What else makes you happy at Christmas?"

Chester used a cloth to grasp the handle of the pan and gave the chestnuts a shake as the boy frowned, thinking. "Well, I always wished to go caroling, but I was never old enough."

Miss Deering looked thoughtful. "We could go about with the group from the church, but that wouldn't truly be fulfilling our mission, would it? We are meant to bring the cheer of Christmas to the house and to the countess. Why do we not plan a small party here? With caroling and wassail? We can ask the servants to take part and friends from the village to come and serenade Lady Chester."

"She would like it?" the boy asked. "If we all sang to her?"

"I should think so. It would be a lovely surprise and a way to start truly feeling the season, don't you think?"

"I like the sound of it," Chester said. And he liked that she kept Lady Chester in the focus of their efforts.

"You could perhaps invite your friend, Nick," Miss Deering told Charlie.

"Who else?" The boy was entering into the spirit of the idea. "Do you still have friends in the village, sir?"

"I do." He thought back to so many of the days of his youth spent here, rather than at his mother's dark, stifling home in Devonshire. "What about you, Miss Deering? Do you have friends in the village you'd care to invite?"

Her expression shuttered. "I have . . . some acquaintances

that I think would like to come, to surprise the dowager countess."

He stilled. Acquaintances were not the same as friends. Had she no—

"Listen," Miss Deering said suddenly, cocking her head. "Do you hear something?"

Chester looked toward the door. Visitors?

But the girl was leaning toward the fire. "It sounds like it's coming from here." She knelt down and leaned in.

Chester started forward. "Perhaps you should—"

Pop! The loud noise came from the fire.

Pop! Pop!

Chester jerked. Charlie jumped. Miss Deering let out a yelp and scooted away from the hearth. He dropped down and grabbed her shoulders, turning her to face him. "Are you all right?"

She blinked at him and pulled away to brush at her forehead and cheeks.

"Miss Deering?" He stared. Yellowish clumps were scattered across her face.

"Damnation. Have you been burnt?"

"No. No." She looked at him and blinked again. He could see chestnut mush in her lashes. "I don't think I made those cuts deep enough," she said blandly.

A strange sound rose up and out of her. Chester cringed. There were two ways forward here, he mentally predicted. The women he usually associated with would be embarrassed and furious. The typical young gentlewoman would be embarrassed and distraught. Tears or tantrum, neither path would be pleasant. He braced himself as another odd sound burbled out of her.

And then, abruptly, she just . . . dissolved. Sank back onto the floor. He stared, uncomprehending for a moment. Was it a fit?

But, no. She was . . . laughing! More accurately, she was chortling and snorting, holding one hand across her belly while the other wiped at her eye. She took that hand away and pointed at him—and then laughed harder.

Charlie began to laugh.

She pointed again. "You . . . you . . ." She could not catch her breath. "You should see your face!"

Charlie laughed harder.

Chester gave a harrumph. "*My* face?"

But inside of him, that lingering anxiety dissolved. He watched her laughing at herself—and him—with utter abandon and something else bloomed in its stead. Surprise. Interest. Wonder.

Perhaps a bit of longing.

Pop!

Another one went off. They all jumped. There was a moment of silence and then they were all howling with laughter.

It went on for several helpless minutes. At last Chester harnessed enough control to wipe his eyes and remove the pan from the fire.

Miss Deering let out a last few chortles, then climbed to her feet. "Well, then. We've had quite a start to our mission." She chuckled. "I will leave the pleasure of eating and sharing the chestnuts to you two. I've had quite enough." Another snort. "Now, I believe I will go and wash up."

Chester got to his feet as she left and watched her go. All of that good humor left a glow behind, but he suddenly felt quite solemn.

A woman who could laugh at herself? Unheard of. A girl who not only caught his eye, but piqued his interest? A girl who liked animals more than people. One who seemed kindness itself to young Charlie—and earned fervent praises from both his grandmother and Mrs. Jensen—but didn't have friends? Miss Deering had layers. He'd like to peel them all away—and for the first time he wasn't meaning her garments.

But he'd made Grandmama a promise—and truly—Miss Deering was likely too good for the likes of him. He'd promised himself he would take this time to think about his life. To reflect on his choices and decide just what he wanted.

But just now, he couldn't help but wonder what it was she wanted . . .

CHAPTER 5

The ring of the bell startled Julia.

"Goodness, you finished early this morning," she said as she entered the dowager's rooms. Lady Chester was sealing the last of the day's letters.

"Yes. I shared the news of our guests with everyone of importance yesterday. Not so much news to impart today, as I am not inclined to tell the tale of your first experience roasting chestnuts."

An unforeseen chuckle burbled out of her. "No, indeed. I thank you for your discretion."

The dowager stood and moved to a chair closer to the fire. "Would you find my green woolen shawl, Julia? Good heavens, but the cold has grown bitter, hasn't it?"

"It has." Julia draped the wrap over the older woman's shoulders. "Old Starkie, in the stables, swears it is going to snow, later."

"His rheumatism is generally accurate," the countess conceded. "Now, tell me, where are Chester and Charlie?"

"They are bundling up, getting ready to go out and gather greenery for the house."

The dowager looked up. "Eckles won't have it in the house before Christmas Eve."

"Yes. The earl was already aware of that. Plans have been hatched to keep it safely in the tack room and prepare it there, in the meantime."

"That will do." She shot Julia a glance askance. "I'm sorry, but I hope you had not planned to go out with them. I'm afraid I must play the oppressive employer and send you out on errands for me, while I toast my old bones by the fire."

Julia, kneeling to place the countess's footstool in just the right place, smiled up at her. "That's exactly why I am here, my lady. I told them I would be unable to accompany them. We have the servants' boxing day gifts to finish."

"Yes, yes. Do bring me my embroidery. I know I have the easier job of it, doing the men's handkerchiefs, but it was you who insisted on asking about each of the women's favorite flower and embellishing theirs with a representation."

"I know it is a bit of extra work, but I do think it is so nice to get something meant just for you."

"Well, the men will be happy with a simple osprey along with their initials, I do hope. I do not have your skill, and it is a part of the Chester crest, after all."

"I believe they will be very happy with their gifts, indeed."

The pair of them had set up a temporary stillroom in the apple barn this summer. The place was unused at that time of year and the perfect place for the ladies to mix up scented ointments. Lavender and rose water for the women and bergamot and rosemary for the men. Moreland Cottage boasted only a small group of servants, but they were a hard-working and kindly lot and they would each get a small basket with gifts hand made by Julia and the countess, a bit of hard cider made from Moreland's orchards, as well as fresh-baked treats ordered from the village.

"I'd also like to discuss just what you are hoping for, in

giving us this mission to bring Christmas to Moreland," Julia said.

"Yes, yes. It's Christmas at the top of my list for you today. We need presents for both of our guests." The dowager looked toward the window. "Thank the heavens for Mr. Bonneville. It's truly a luxury to have a skilled glover right here in Farduff. Chester quite favors the man's riding gloves. I'll want a good pair—his best. And tell him to add in a pint of his leather pomade, too. Remind him that I like the mixture of yellow ochre with the white pipe clay."

Julia made a note. She also noted how the dowager had sidestepped her question, but she didn't press the matter. "And Charlie?"

"A book. A good, thick one, filled with adventure. That's what boys need to read. He hasn't read Robinson Crusoe yet. I asked. That will do nicely." A crafty grin spread across her face. "And a slingshot, too."

Julia looked up and raised a brow.

"Yes. I said it and I meant it. Perhaps the child will break something. I hope he does. That one needs to learn how to make a mistake—and to trust that the world won't end if he does. How can he learn anything if he's too afraid to make a mistake?"

"I think he needs to learn to trust us, ma'am," Julia ventured.

"And what better way than to make a mess and be reassured?"

"Perhaps you are right," she said thoughtfully. She was entirely sympathetic with the boy's wariness. But she hoped he would decide to put his faith in them. His great-grandmother would certainly not disappoint him, and she would do her best for him, as well.

"Of course, I am right." The dowager paused. "There's something else."

"Yes?"

"I would like you to look for a box. A fine one, if there's one to be had. Nothing too flowery or feminine, as it's for Chester. About the size of a cigar box, I'd say, but made of wood and meant to last. It's for a special gift."

"I will scour the village, my lady."

"I know you will." She leaned toward the warmth of the fire, but watched Julia as she asked, "So. What do you think of Lord Chester?"

Julia considered her answer. "I think he is . . . large. And I do not mean only in the physical sense."

The countess cackled. "He does have shoulders like an ox, doesn't he? But I do know what you mean to say. That boy is large in body and spirit—and in his zest for life." Sitting back, she grew sober. "I suppose all young men must rebel. It is the way of things. The problem is, though, that the boy thinks living a loud, licentious life is the answer, when true rebellion would just be for him to live happily." She sighed. "Ah, well. It's in the blood, I suppose. I had quite a wild time of it myself, when I was young."

"You, ma'am?" Julia pretended to be shocked.

"Indeed. We were not so prim and proper as you lot, when I was young. Nor so dull, I daresay. We flirted madly and loved with gusto. We yearned and wrote poetry and drove each other to excess. I had more than one duel fought over me, I don't mind telling you."

"Goodness." Julia couldn't imagine being a part of any of those things.

The dowager pointed toward the carved mantel and the set of books that held a place of honor there. "We made those stories seem tame," she said proudly. *The Lattimere Legends* had been a sensation years earlier, the tales of a society girl who lived an adventurous, secret life. The *beau monde* had been scandalized and titillated with the notion that it was all true and based on the diaries of a young girl of the *ton*. Lady Chester was proud of her first editions.

"Do you think it's true that Lord Carnham's younger son was the author? That he used a female perspective to hide his identity?" Julia asked, fascinated.

The dowager countess's gaze had unfocused. "It must have been someone from our set. We all had our theories."

"Do you think they were really true, as so many others did?"

"They have the ring of truth in them. I did recognize several of the incidents described in the tales." Lady Chester shook her head. "In any case, that was all before I met my beloved Chester. What a man he was! And with him I discovered the true adventure of life." She sat silent for a moment, with her eyes closed. They opened suddenly, and she looked toward the door.

"My grandson, too, will eventually discover there is more to life than *sturm und drang*," she continued. "He's made a start, with those friends of his. They watch over him and keep him from crossing the line. He'll find the path to real happiness eventually." She pointed her finger at Julia. "But he's not on it yet. Don't let him make you one of his flirts along the way, my girl. The world takes a dim view of such things now, and you don't have the same standing that I did, back then."

Julia blushed furiously. "I don't think there's any danger of that, my lady."

"Well, it's just as well. Now, you head into the village and act as my Christmas messenger, will you? And come up for a gossip when you get back."

Julia bit back a smile. "Yes, my lady."

She left to fetch her wrap, but she couldn't help but wonder what exactly Lord Chester's loud, wildly licentious life might entail.

CHARLIE WATCHED Miss Deering as she headed for her room. He jumped when the dowager's sharp voice called out. "I know you are lurking out there. I heard your step. Come on in, then."

Trying not to look guilty, he slunk inside and gave his great-grandmother a bow.

"Well?" Her brow raised, she waited.

"Lord Chester sent me to see if you needed anything, before we head out to the woods, ma'am."

"Not a thing, thank you. Except . . ."

He waited.

"I need you to relax and enjoy yourself, eh?"

He smiled. "Yes, ma'am."

"And since you were undeniably listening . . . about that question you asked me yesterday . . ."

"Yes?"

"A prime strategy for helping two young people realize they wish to be together . . ."

"Yes?"

"Is to tell them they must remain apart." She laughed. "Now, go on with you."

Grinning, he bowed and left.

CHESTER DROVE SLOWLY on the thin track through the woods. The farm cart was piled high with laurel, holly, rosemary and evergreen fir. They had more than enough to deck all the halls at Moreland, but inside his head, he kept hearing Miss Deering and both the eagerness and hesitation she'd exhibited when she requested the greenery. Something told him it was a part of Christmas she'd never experienced—and longed to. The thought was a forlorn one. It struck him in the chest every time he was about to declare they had enough —and he would push on to search for more.

Besides, they were missing the most important bit of all.

"Keep your eyes sharp," he told Charlie, beside him on the bench of the cart. "Look for a big ash or a hawthorn tree. That's where we'll find mistletoe."

"Mistletoe?" Charlie made a face. "Do we need it?"

"Indeed, we do." The vision hung in his mind for a moment—Julia Deering in his arms under a kissing bough. She was taller than his usual flirts and dalliances tended to be. He rather thought he would enjoy having her curves pressed against him in new and interesting places and her lips easily in reach for—

"For kisses?" Charlie gave another grimace.

"For *Christmas* kisses, which are special."

"How?"

He shrugged. "They hold a spark of Christmas magic in them, I suppose."

The boy looked thoughtful. Nodding, he dutifully peered into the trees as they passed and several minutes later, he was the one to call out. "Isn't that an ash?"

The tree was a good way from the track. "Let's see." Chester tied the horses and they went to investigate.

"Well spotted, Charlie," he said with approval. "I daresay you'll be an eagle eye, like your father. He could pick out a grouse hiding in the bush before the dogs could scent them."

"Could he?" The boy looked entranced. "Was he a good shot, as well?"

"The best." Chester usually made it a point not to talk about or dwell on the past, but the boy was hungry for information about his father. He could scarcely blame him.

"I'm the best at archery, amongst the boys at Mr. Rule's." Going suddenly pale, Charlie pressed his lips together.

"Have you learned to shoot yet?"

"No, sir." He was definitely subdued now.

Chester turned to face him. "Charlie, I know about Rule. Are you worried about where you'll go from here?"

The boy looked at the ground.

"There's no need for worry. We will find the right situation for you. I want you to live in a place where you can learn much, laugh more, roam a bit and enjoy your boyhood. We'll search together."

Charlie didn't answer, so Chester turned his attention to the tree. "Yes—look up high—there's a crown of mistletoe up there." He began swinging his arms to warm up the muscles.

"How will we get it down?"

"I'll climb up."

He did, although he had Charlie toss him a long branch so he could tease a large clump of the vine from the high, thin branches.

Jumping down, he brushed his hands off. "Now we can head back."

Charlie stood waiting, his arms full. As they loaded it in with the rest of the greenery, the boy spoke up. "Sir?"

"Yes?"

"Can we *not* tell Grandmama and Miss Deering about Mr. Rule? Not until later?"

Chester grimaced. "I fear the countess already knows."

"Oh." The boy sounded suddenly small.

Chester bent down to look him in the eye. "Charlie—you know you did nothing wrong? Mr. Rule made wrong choices, but they were nothing to do with you."

"Oh, I know."

Chester sighed. "We can avoid the subject until after the holiday, if you like."

Charlie looked up. "Thank you, sir."

Together they secured the load and set out to return to

Moreland. Charlie held silent for a while, but suddenly he straightened his shoulders. "I wonder if I could ask another favor, sir?"

"Of course."

The boy cleared his throat. "I would like to give Grandmama and Miss Deering gifts at Christmas."

"Oh, well, I've just sent for some things. Something particular for the countess. And a friend of mine sponsors a small enterprise, making lavender lotions and sachets and other womanly type notions. I've sent for some of their products. They can count as coming from the two of us."

The boy held his stiff position. "The ladies have been good to me, sir. I would like to do something for them. Something from me, alone. Unfortunately, I do not have any funds. Perhaps you might loan me a small amount? I swear, I'll pay you back, somehow. I can run errands for you, or even for people in the village. Perhaps make deliveries for the mercantile—"

Chester waved for him to stop. "No funds," he repeated. Run errands? Make deliveries? His heart dropped as he thought back. He'd arranged with Rule for Charlie's education, his care and room and board. Had the agreement not included a bit of spending money for the lad? He couldn't recall—which likely meant it had not. His jaw tightened. He just had not put himself in the boy's place enough to consider it. He'd been too concerned with his own pleasures and he'd unwittingly failed the child—again. He could not go on like this. "Good heavens, lad. You should have had a quarterly allowance. I'll arrange it right away and advance you funds now—and don't think of paying back what you should already have had."

Relief showed clear on the lad's face. "Thank you, sir." He was struck suddenly. "But what should I get for them—the ladies? I'd like for it to be a special gift—meant just for each of them."

Chester liked the lad's generous impulses. He also recognized opportunity when it dropped in his lap. "Well, we shall have to do a bit of sleuthing, won't we?"

"I'd get Miss Deering a sword, if I could. One like Boudicca fought with. I know she'd like that, but Mrs. Eckles said it wasn't appropriate for a lady."

"No, likely it's not," Chester said, hiding a grin. "But we shall ask some questions. Discover their likes and dislikes. I have a good idea of Grandmother's tastes, but none at all of Miss Deering's." Beyond a bloodthirsty appreciation of Celtic history, apparently.

All of his conundrums were coming to roost together—but suddenly he didn't mind. He must begin looking beyond himself—and starting with Miss Deering would be no hardship. She seemed kind—and skilled at knowing how to care for others. Perhaps he could learn from her—and about her at the same time.

The afternoon sun was sinking when the track they followed let them out on the main road, although they'd left through the orchards. Chester turned toward Moreland and they were nearly at the turning onto the estate when Charlie suddenly stiffened in his seat.

"Sir! Chester, that is, I see a friend ahead in the road. Would you mind if I run to catch him?"

"Not at all." Chester saw only the portly form of an older gentleman ahead, moving in the direction of the village, but he stopped to let the boy down and turned his head to watch Charlie disappear around the bend in the road after him. Shrugging, he urged the horse toward the stables, where he saw all the greenery carefully unloaded into the tack room. Here there was a long table, a chair and a bench, all which would be useful as they wrestled the greenery into garlands and boughs.

He left it all piled there as he gave the gelding a good brushing, then broke off a piece of pommage left over from the apple harvesting, to offer in thanks. The stable lads had gone to their midday meal and all lay quiet now. On his way out he paused before a smaller, empty stall. Leaning over the half door, he stared inside, letting memory wash over him.

He didn't know how much time passed before someone spoke behind him, making him jump.

"The place is a lot quieter without him, but I'm darned if I don't miss the old rascal."

"Starkie." Chester greeted the old stablemaster and gripped his shoulder. "It's good to see you. Did you hide when you saw me roll in with a full cart?"

"Didn't have to. I'm no fool. I let the young ones do the heavy work around here, these days. They are all right excited about the greenery, in any case." He lifted a brow. "I'll expect you have brought back enough to deck out the servant's quarters?"

"Did you doubt it? Yes, there is plenty to go around."

Starkie nodded. "I told them it would be so." He nodded toward the empty stall. "There are a couple of boys here now that never knew Old Henry."

"Sometimes I wish I hadn't."

"I wouldn't blame you, if you meant that, but I know you don't. Even if he was the most cantankerous old ass that ever graced God's green earth."

The old man was right, he supposed.

"How long?" Starkie asked quietly.

Chester raised a brow.

"How long did Ensign last, after you came and fetched him back with you?"

"A few months. But I made sure they were good ones." He sighed. "I swear, that dog taught me how to be a good man."

"He taught us all a few lessons," the old stablemaster said gruffly. "Some animals are good people."

"Speaking of good people—tell me about Miss Deering."

The old man shot him a sharp glance. "Is she a good one? Is that what you are asking?"

Chester nodded.

"The best. You may lay your worries over that."

He met the man's gaze. "Truly?"

"Hand to God," Starkie vowed. "She's been good for the dowager countess. In truth, she's been good for all of us. It was damned quiet when Old Henry and Ensign were both gone, but it grew sad and sorry without the apple harvesting."

Chester stared. "Without the harvesting?"

"Aye. Did you not know?"

"No," he answered, alarm and anger growing.

Starkie sighed. "Old Henry was gone and then you and Ensign were, as well. The dowager is growing older. She just . . . lost the heart for it all. And so it was . . . abandoned. Two seasons with no picking, no singing. No bonfires when the orchard was stripped. No rivalries in the kitchen over who made the best dumplings, no horse mill, no cider pressing, none of it. It took the spark right out of the place, too."

Chester flinched. Another knife, driven deep and twisted hard. That's what this news was. How much had he missed in his selfish drive to grab all of the fun and gaiety and pleasure that had once been denied him?

But, wait. Silently, Chester gestured toward the slatted box where he'd foraged from the cake of pommage.

"Aye. It's back now. It was Miss Deering who brought it back, once she heard of it. First, she brought the dowager out of the doldrums and then she breathed life back into rest of the place."

Chester and the stablemaster stared at each other. Truths passed between them without words.

"Thank you, Starkie."

The old man nodded.

Chester strode out and headed for another uncomfortable interview with his grandmother.

CHAPTER 6

Julia's errands were mostly accomplished with ease. At the glover's, she ran her finger over the soft leather of the riding gloves. So much leather. His hands were large. Strong. She didn't know why the thought made her flush, but she distracted herself with the image of how the earl's blue eyes would crinkle up with his smile when he opened them. She had a fleeting wish that she could inspire such a reaction, but it was in no way appropriate for her to exchange gifts with him.

She had no such compunction about giving Charlie a gift, however, and did not hesitate to add one to her purchases, paid for with her own savings. She also stopped in at the milliner's shop to ask about the crest for the boy's Roman helmet.

Mrs. Laudon was intrigued by the problem and eventually concluded that horsehair must be the best option. "I'll tell you what, if you leave the helmet with me, I'll do it for you. There is a bit of an increase in custom, with the holidays coming, and I have the notion that mothers might see it and wish to purchase one for their own sons."

Julia readily agreed and promised to send the helmet that same day.

That left only her last task, and it proved to be more difficult.

Mr. Bonneville had nothing like a decorative wooden box. She tried Graves' mercantile but could find nothing close. Both Roland and his father appeared to be—made sure to be—too busy to help her with a further suggestion, so she left the shop with a sigh.

Heading for the green, she took a seat on the bench and drew out a handful of invitations to the Christmas Eve wassail party. She'd been discreetly handing them out as she could. Shuffling through them now gave her an idea. Plucking one out, she got to her feet and headed for the far edge of the village.

"Good afternoon, Mr. Haskins!" She raised her hems out of the sawdust as she stepped into the open shed attached to the cooperage.

"Good day to you, Miss Deering." The cooper left off shaping a barrel stave and tugged at his forelock.

She held out the invitation. "We'd love to have you and your wife to a small gathering at Moreland Cottage on Christmas Eve, before the church services."

Smiling, he accepted the offering. "Won't my Etta be thrilled? Thank you, Miss. We'd be delighted."

Julia liked the cooper's young wife. They'd struck up an after-church friendship talking about local plants. "Please ask her to be discreet, though. We mean to surprise the dowager countess with a group of friends and a chorus of Christmas carols."

"Ah. Won't that be grand? We'll keep your secret."

"I have another mission, sir, that I'd like to consult you on." She explained about the box. "You are skilled with wood, and I thought perhaps you might be able to fashion what Lady Chester is looking for?"

He made a face. "Well, I do have a lovely stack of walnut wood. I got it in so I could work on a wardrobe for Etta this winter, when business is slow."

"The dowager countess would certainly pay to replace the wood you used."

"Yes, and I've no doubt of that, but I'm not sure how much decoration I could accomplish, if I'm to make a quality job of it before Christmas."

"I don't think it needs so many flourishes, as long as it is sturdy and well-made." She frowned, thinking. An idea began flitting around in her head. "Mr. Haskins, what if I lined it with rich fabric? I have a lovely, dark green silk that might do."

"That would dress it up," he agreed.

Her enthusiasm grew. "Perhaps I could even embroider a panel for the inside lid?"

He nodded. "My wife greatly admires your skill with a needle, Miss. I'm sure you could do a good job of it."

Julia flushed. "You must send her my thanks for her kind words. But I'm afraid I've only just met the earl. I have no notion of his likes and dislikes. I wouldn't know what to depict."

The cooper grinned. "I've known his lordship for a great many years. We ran around this village as boys—it was always Chester and Mr. Edgerton and me. He is a simple man, sure enough. He likes a lark. He keeps a book in his pocket, always. He tells a fine story, likes a drink, a good song and a wo—" He stopped, looking sheepish. "A wooden box."

She laughed.

He grinned right back. "I do believe I can come up with something to please the countess and his lordship, and I'll get it done in time for you to line it, too, Miss."

"Thank you. You've given me something to work on. A bottle perhaps, and an open book—do you perchance know his favorite book?"

"We never did discuss much literature. But you ask him yourself, Miss. Lord Chester is easy to talk to." He laughed out loud. "He'll likely answer any question a pretty lady like you puts to him, as long as you don't ask him about his family or his younger days." His grin widened. "And whatever you do, don't tease him about his donkey."

She blinked. "Thank you, Mr. Haskins. I believe I can manage to follow your advice."

THE DOWAGER COUNTESS was closeted with the earl when Julia returned to Moreland, so she tucked the purchases away and sent the last few invitations out with the footman. Then she set to work on Charlie's King Arthur inspired costume for the theatrical. She'd already cut out the dragon shape and put a few embroidered touches on it to give it some life. She quickly had it appliqued to the tunic and was just shaking it out when Charlie came in.

She held her small mirror so that he could admire himself in it. His enthusiasm for the project was growing and it warmed her heart to see him coming out of his quiet, unassuming shell a little.

"Lady Chester said she had a capelet that would give me a bit of a look of royalty," he said happily. "And Susan and I are to rummage in one of the costume trunks in the attic for a crown."

"You'll look grand. Now, how is the poem going?"

"I have it nearly memorized. Shall I say it for you?"

"Yes, but why don't we go out and get started on the greenery while we do it?"

The boy was eager to go along.

"Let me get a bag of supplies together and I'll meet you out there. You can sort the different types of greenery, to get started."

An hour later, she was settled comfortably in the tack room in the stables. She'd spent some time teaching Charlie how to weave a garland together and she'd made several bows from the length of red ribbon she'd purchased in the village. Charlie worked on with the greenery and practiced his recital of *The Grave of King Arthur* while she listened and put the finishing touches on her gift for Lady Chester. Once she was done with this, she could begin on a panel to line the earl's Christmas box.

The room was bare but warm. Charlie chattered cheerfully, and she felt cozy and content, though the fir was making her eyes water. Abruptly, the door opened, and Lord Chester came in—and contentment turned to sizzling awareness. All of the nerves under her skin jumped to attention, turning in anticipation toward him like flowers in the sun.

"Here's where the two of you hid away." He wore an odd, contemplative look, the most serious expression she'd yet seen on him. The bold angles of his face seemed sharper, somehow.

"Oh, I should go in to see to Lady Chester," she said, starting to rise.

"No need, not just yet. She had just set Susan to restocking her writing desk and was fussing over it when I left her." He turned toward Charlie. "At work already? Good lad." The earl carried an ornate goblet. He saluted the boy with it and took a drink.

"I'm making a long garland for the stairs," Charlie told him.

"I'll join you and start in on the other end." He settled on the bench next to the boy and set his goblet away from the greenery.

"Do you need Miss Deering to teach you?"

The earl's laugh sounded uncomfortably bitter. "I fear I need Miss Deering to teach me a great many things. But garland? I am an old hand at that."

He began to idly weave laurel and rosemary together and took another long swig from the cup.

Julia sank back in her seat. The small room seemed to have shrunk significantly, with the earl's larger-than-life presence. She shouldn't stare. Not at his tawny hair or pensive, blue eyes or how the cut of his coat emphasized the way his wide chest narrowed to his waist. She stared at his cup, instead, and was suddenly inspired. The goblet was large and made of metal, with a wide base, a thin stem and a basin covered with a gorgeously complicated, scrolling design.

"Would you like me to fetch you a drink, Miss Deering?" he asked wryly.

She flushed and looked back down to the work in her lap. "No, indeed. I'm sorry. I was only fascinated with your goblet. I've never seen it before and it is beautiful, indeed."

"It was a gift, a set given to my grandfather by the king, long before His Majesty succumbed to madness. It fascinated me as a child. Grandpapa always let me drink from it. Now, Mrs. Eckles keeps it tucked away in the butler's pantry, but she takes it out for me, when I visit."

"That is a lovely memory and a nice tradition." It would be perfect for her embroidered panel. And on that subject . . . "Do you perhaps have a book in your pocket, sir?"

He looked surprise. "Yes. Why do you ask?"

"It's just something Mr. Haskins mentioned—that you always carry a book in your pocket."

Charlie looked interested. "Do you, sir?"

"I do."

"Why?"

"In case I find myself waiting or bored or just quiet—and can find a chance to read."

"What are you reading now, my lord?" Julia asked.

"*Marmion*." He grinned. "All that scheming and lus—" He glanced at Charlie. "Longing."

She bit back a grin. "Ah, yes, a bit of light, holiday reading."

He shot her a heated look. "Some things are appropriate year-round." Adding a bit more greenery to his end of the strand, he inclined his head toward her lap. "And what is it you are working on, instead of our Christmas project?"

"A Christmas project of my own—a gift for the dowager countess."

"What is it?" Charlie asked, perking up again.

"It's a mantle. She admired my cloak, so I'm making a version of it for her, except the embroidery is inspired by the Chester coat of arms."

"Ah, yes. I see. Ospreys perched on the vines and cinque-foil flowers?" The earl took another drink. His blue eyes flashed at her. "Your skill with a needle is undeniable, but so apparently, is the thoughtfulness of your nature."

She blushed uncertainly. His tone was weighted down with irony and it didn't sound *completely* like a compliment.

"I want to give great grandmama a gift," Charlie said. "Something she will like very well, but I don't have any ideas what it could be."

Julia pursed her lips. "Do you know, I'd wager you might have an idea."

"I do?"

"Just think about it. You've been here long enough to see how Lady Chester spends her days. What have you seen that makes her happy?"

"A bit of brandy in her tea?"

She tried not to laugh. "Yes, but something else, perhaps?"

The boy considered. "When letters come in the post?"

"Exactly. So why do you not write her a letter? Tell her what you've enjoyed about Moreland and your stay here?"

"And she'd like that? Better than something dressed up with a bow?" He sounded doubtful.

"I believe she would," she answered firmly. "Now." She cut the last thread and stood up, shaking out the ivory mantle and swinging it about her shoulders. "It's finished." She ran her fingers down the green, brown and gold embroidery. "What do you think?"

"It's pretty," Charlie admitted. "Are you sure a letter will be as good as that?"

"The letter will be better, because it comes from your heart," she told him.

He sighed. "If you say so."

"We must take Miss Deering's advice," Lord Chester said. "As she's modeling such a lovely gift and has given you a generous suggestion, we must assume she's come by her wisdom with experience. Surely she's been given more than a few excellent gifts herself."

Julia stiffened. Disappointment wrenched through her. "No," she said sharply. "If you take any of my advice, Charlie, let it be this. Do *not* make assumptions." She lifted her chin. "And never speak or act on them as if you know them to be true."

CHESTER BLINKED. So, Miss Deering was not all softness and light. She looked fierce as she stood over the boy, still swathed in her beautiful creation. He almost expected her to whip it around Charlie like a shield, to protect him from Chester's bad advice.

"Whyever not?" he asked. Taking another drink, he slammed the goblet down. "People's low assumptions definitely make my life easier."

"Do they?" She raised a brow and tilted her head toward the boy.

He flushed. "Well, perhaps until recently." But that wasn't true, either, was it? Not after all he'd learned today.

Charlie stood. Looking between them, he began to sidle toward the door. "I think I'll head in and ask Susan to help me find that crown."

The girl swung the mantle from her shoulders and began to stuff her supplies into a bag. "I'll be following right behind you."

Charlie left and Chester stood and went to hold her bag so Miss Deering could pack away her threads and sundries. "I apologize if I upset you."

"I would only be upset if Charlie believed such things to be acceptable."

He closed the bag and met her gaze directly. "I'm sorry if I pricked a nerve. I take you have not received a great many gifts, then?"

"One. I received one gift, in the entirety of my life before I came to Moreland, but I've been on the receiving end of many more painful assumptions."

"I'm sorry to hear it. Who has judged you harshly, without reason?"

She gave a bitter laugh and tried to pull her bag away from him. "Who hasn't?"

"You're not comfortable sharing a painful moment from your past? You certainly witnessed one of my worst moments the other night." He ruefully touched the back of his head. "And patched me up after it, too."

"I would prefer not to," she said wryly.

"Oh, come now. I've been hoping for a chance to get to know you better."

"Why? So you can ferret out the truth about me? So you can be sure I am not taking advantage of Lady Chester or doing her some harm? Because I can assure you, you wouldn't be the first to make those *false assumptions*."

He winced. "I already know how good you are for my grandmother. It didn't take long to discover that truth. And today I learned how you brought the apple harvest back to Moreland. It's an important part of the year here, a highlight in the rhythm of the heart of the place. I'm grateful to you for it."

Her scowl faded. "Lady Chester has been just as good for me."

"I'm glad. But honestly, I was hoping to learn more about you for my own selfish reasons."

It was true. His relationships with women had mostly been casual and temporary. He'd moved from one to the other with ease, until Deliah—and look how incredibly wrong he's been with her.

Julia Deering was different. The more he learned about her, the more she seemed to exude wisdom and kindness. He ached to soak it up, to delve deeper and discover where it came from. She was pretty, all of his straining senses could attest to it, with that creamy skin and those dark eyes and rare, blinding smiles. Whatever it was she emanated into the world, he was like a hungry boy with his nose pressed against the bakery glass, wanting it.

He met her gaze frankly. "I've practically cultivated low assumptions and expectations. I've had reasons for it. But, standing in that inn, knowing I'd failed that boy . . ." He swallowed and shook his head. "I was standing there, waiting to hear if the proprietor could track down the name of the woman who had taken Charlie on, or what her final destination had been. Two women passed as I stood there, praying with all of my might that I might find the boy. One of them asked who I was and remarked upon my looks. Her friend glanced over and shrugged. "Oh, that's Lord Chester. Turn away, dear, nothing there but excellent tailoring wrapped about empty space."

Miss Deering looked shocked—and endearingly indignant. Her reaction was a balm—and he craved more.

"Last week I would have laughed. I would have repeated her remark to all of my friends and hoped it reached my . . . certain others. But hearing it while that boy's welfare hung in the balance?" It had been a pain made worse by all he'd discovered in the last days. "I need a change, I believe. And perhaps, a friend."

He took her bag and set it aside, then took her hand. It was warm and soft—save for the hard calluses left by her needles. An immediate image of those small hands roving over him invaded his brain. He could imagine the contrast—

"You have friends still, here in the village, sir."

Swallowing, he chased the vision away. "None so suited to help me become a better man, I suspect."

Her gaze softened, and Chester didn't hesitate to press his point.

"I have a confession to make, Miss Deering."

She peered up at him through her lashes and he almost forgot to continue, he was so caught by the pull of those dark eyes—

"Sir?"

"Yes. You see, I arrived in Farduff a couple of days ago thinking I might never trust another woman. In truth, the dowager countess is the only woman in the entirety of my life who has never let me down."

She nodded. "I felt much the same when I arrived, except

I felt that way about . . . everyone. Your grandmother has given me a bit of faith in humanity again."

"And yet, you are still wary with most people, are you not?"

"Yes," she whispered.

"I propose we strike a bargain. You trust Grandmama, as do I. And she appears to trust us both. Why do we not, then, decide to take the risk and trust each other?"

She pulled her hand away.

"It's the holiday season, Miss Deering. Perhaps it's the perfect time for us both to take a leap of faith."

She took a deep breath. Looking up, she searched his face, and at last, gave a nod.

He grinned in relief. "I thank you for taking a chance on me."

"I believe you do wish for . . . something different." She sighed. "And I don't have so many friends that I can afford to toss your offer away."

"Very well, then. I will assure you that I do make a decent friend. I promise to be easy-going and I won't demand heart-to-heart discussions or ask personal questions."

She tilted her head. "But isn't that what friendship is? Learning about and coming to appreciate one another?"

"I appreciate you already. But if you feel the need to tell me the tale of those painful assumptions—then I will gladly side with you and help you get a bit of your own back."

She shook her head. "It's all over and done with now."

"Perhaps." He grinned. "But perhaps you merely need an inventive mind at your disposal."

She bit her lip. "I begin to suspect you are incorrigible, my lord."

"Oh, that's no great deduction," he said cheerfully. "Everyone knows that." He pulled out the chair. "Now, would you care to take a seat and begin?"

Shaking her head, she took up her bag again. "No. I shall tell you, if you wish to know, but another time. The dowager will be needing me, and it won't do to spend too long a time out here, alone."

He let her go then, satisfied that she would keep her word. But could she do it? Could she teach him to be a better man, a better friend? And would he, at last, become the sort of man a woman might wish to count on?

IT WAS VERY LATE, or very early, perhaps. Either way, Charlie could not remember ever being awake at such an hour—with sunrise still more than an hour away. Susan had awakened him, however, because she had agreed to help with his latest attempt at matchmaking.

He slipped out of the house, to the stables, past the horses still sleeping in their stalls, and into the tack room. The sharp smell of evergreen chased the last cobwebs from his brain. It only took a short while for him to create a small but pretty garland of mixed greens for a mantle, another smaller one for a headboard and a couple of small loops to encircle a candlestick or lamp.

He didn't know much about young ladies, but Charlie knew yearning. He'd recognized it in Miss Deering's tone when she spoke of greenery in the house, and he'd seen the excitement in her eyes when she first spied the bundles of fronds, branches and vines they'd brought back. Nick had told him that couples in love often did nice things for one another, and Charlie had immediately formulated this plan. Miss Deering could awake to the surprise of her own private greenery—and Mrs. Eckles surely would not object if it was in but one room of the house—and if she thought the earl had arranged it.

Susan had agreed that everyone, Miss Deering included, would think it Lord Chester's idea. Charlie had approached the countess's lady's maid as the logical choice to help him and she'd been delighted with the idea. She could accomplish it, she assured him, because she'd started out in service as a young girl, the lowest on the ladder, and the one who had to creep into rooms before dawn to light the morning fires. "I learned to move in and out with scarcely a sound, lest I get a pillow—or a boot—tossed at me."

Susan also promised to say only, if questioned, that she'd been recruited by someone who cared. Charlie thought that if Miss Deering thought the earl cared enough to arrange such a surprise, then she would surely look at him in the same light—and they might begin to do more than watch each other avidly when the other wasn't looking.

He felt like he must try something. The cooking plan had well, exploded. He grinned, just thinking of it. At least they had all been able to laugh about it. Lady Chester's idea of forbidding them to like each other just didn't feel right. But this? It felt . . . thoughtful. Like her.

Feeling hopeful, he gathered up an armful of greenery and headed for the servant's entrance at the back of the house. Peering carefully over the foliage, he was nearly there when he caught a whiff of smoke over the balsam scent of his burden.

"Now, then. What's this?"

The orange tip of a cheroot glared in the dark. Charlie stopped and peered into the gloom—and was shocked to recognize Mr. Roland Graves leaning against a pile of crates. "What are you doing here?"

Graves shrugged. "I had a . . . late delivery for Ruby."

"The kitchen maid? But why are you still here, then?"

The man chuckled. "We got a little involved in our . . . conversation."

"Oh." Charlie moved on again, but suddenly stopped. "Are you Ruby's beau?"

Grave ground his cheroot under his heel. "I suppose so, of a sort. Certainly, she'd like to think so."

"How did you get her to like you?"

"Well, and is that what this is all about?" The man gestured. "You are young for it, but are you looking at one of the—oh, but no! You've got a *tendre* for the companion, haven't you?"

"What? No!" Charlie scoffed.

"There's no shame in admitting it, boy. She's easy to look at and has curves in all the right places—but do not let your hopes climb too high." He bent down and Charlie saw his lip curl. "That one has her eye to the main chance, don't she? And I'm sure she's set her gaze on the unmarried earl in the house."

Charlie hoped she had—but he did not like the disdainful way Graves spoke of it. "Do not say a bad word about Miss Deering!" he warned.

"Oh, and won't I? After she dealt me a nasty turn, interfering in matters and re-starting Moreland's harvest? Do you know the profit she cost me? I had them picked for a song and made a bundle selling them on to the city grocers. Fools were willing to pay extra for fruit from a *countess's* orchard." He gave a nasty moan. "I miss that tidy sum. She took it from me, and I'll vent my spleen to anyone who will listen."

Charlie tightened his grip until a jagged edge of holly pierced his skin. He'd been in the general store when Graves, and other members of his family, were spreading gossip. Everyone shopped there, from the village and from the surrounding countryside. The man could do serious damage to Miss Deering's reputation.

He frowned. Neither Graves nor the villagers would

listen to a boy. He lifted his chin and narrowed his eyes. "You do that," he said quietly.

"And I'll see what the earl has to say about it."

Turning on his heel, he continued on into the house and up the stairs to where Susan waited.

Julia woke with a start. Had she heard something? The snick of a door closing? It was still dark, though. She listened, but the house lay quiet, so far as she could tell. The wind blew fiercely outside, though. Perhaps that was the noise she heard.

Rolling over, she tried to get comfortable again. It was likely just her worries jolting her awake. Worries and restless dreams of large hands, soft whispers, blue eyes and muscled backs.

With a groan, she turned again. She had no business having such dreams. Or harboring such thoughts. Or giving way to yearning, fretful *hope*.

She knew better. Experience had taught her better. Lord Chester was a titled nobleman known for his wild habits and rakish ways. Though he had so far been respectful of her status as an upper servant in his grandmother's home. He might turn out to be the first man of her acquaintance, not related to her, who did not expect something inappropriate and turn ugly when he didn't get it. He might indeed be at a crossroads in his life and in need of friendly ear to talk him through it—but it would never amount to more and she just shouldn't entertain any other notion.

Closing her eyes, she tried to doze again. She drifted in and out, but still kept hearing the rumble of the earl's laughter, feeling the race of her heart when his warm hand took hers, and smelling the tang of evergreen that had lingered about them in the tack room.

She didn't know how long she lay there before she realized thickening congestion was making it difficult to breathe, but dawn lit the room when she sat up, reaching for a handkerchief.

She froze. The soft light illuminated the mixed garland that adorned her mantel. More greenery circled the candle stick by her bed and draped above her, along her simple headboard.

Oh! What a lovely surprise! Her heart melted even as her nose began to run. Had the earl done this? She'd seen him watching her closely as they discussed how to bring Christmas to the house. She blinked her stinging eyes and just as she noticed the heavy amount of fir amongst the garlands above her head, she began to sneeze.

Good heavens. Eyes watering, she dashed for the window, threw it open, stuck her head out and gulped in the cold, fresh, clean air. She glanced back, still touched. It was a lovely surprise, even if her congested head could not appreciate it.

Shivering, she turned back and reached for her dressing gown. A large sneeze caught her—and then once she started, she couldn't stop. Nose streaming, she headed for the door. It swung open and Susan stood there, aghast.

"Oh, Miss!" She looked horrified.

"It's fine," she said thickly, blowing her nose and moving toward the door. "I'm fine." She sneezed again. "It's just the fir. It makes me . . . *Achoo! Achoo!*"

"Yes," the maid said wryly. "So I see."

Wiping her eyes, Julia emerged into the passageway. A little way down, the dowager countess stepped out, frowning and pushing her nightcap away from her face. "What's this? What's the commotion?"

A door slammed from further away and the earl came around the corner.

Julia sneezed and frantically wiped at her eyes. Lord Chester was striding down the corridor, clad only in a pair of tight breeches, with a banyan-type dressing gown unbelted and flowing out behind him. Her heart stopped, then *thumped, thumped, thumped* into an unsteady gallop. *Good heavens*. He was . . . He looked . . . She blinked again, furiously, unable to look away, unwilling to miss a moment's glimpse of broad shoulders or bare, expansive chest. Her gaze traveled on to his narrow waist and the tight stretch of fabric over muscled thighs—

"What is it?" He stopped to look at Julia and she hid her running nose behind her kerchief. "Your eyes are red. Is it your fire? Is it smoking?" He strode past her into the room and she hurriedly blew her nose.

Lord Chester came back out. He moved close and looked her over. "Is it the fir?" he asked.

She nodded. Fighting to keep her eyes on his face, she folded her handkerchief and opened her mouth to answer— and let out instead, an explosive, massive sneeze—all over his bare chest.

She froze.

He froze.

Susan covered her mouth.

The dowager countess sniggered.

Someone let out a long, horrified gasp. It was Charlie, peering from the stairwell.

Why wasn't the floor opening to swallow her up? "Oh, my

—I am so sorry, sir!" Reaching out, she began to wipe his chest. His warm, broad, heavily muscled chest.

He made a sound and she looked up into his strained face and realized she was using her damp handkerchief.

The dowager countess cleared her throat. "Step away, dear, and do stop mauling my grandson. He can see to himself."

She stepped back, sneezed again, and blushed with what must be a thousand shades of red as the earl pulled the robe closed around him and Lady Chester stepped to her doorway and peered inside.

"Well, then. I see. In all, it was a nice gesture." The dowager countess peered from Julia to the earl and on to Charlie, who looked distraught. She sighed and motioned to Susan. "Well, call up the maids and clear it out."

"No!" Julia stepped forward. She looked pleadingly at Susan. "Could you have them just remove the fir? The laurel and holly and rosemary don't bother me and it's just so lovely. I do appreciate such a thoughtful surprise, even if my wretched nose does not."

Susan looked to the dowager countess.

"Very well. Take one of the guest rooms until yours is aired out." The dowager countess moved toward her own room. "There will be no sleeping now. We might as well make a morning of it." She pointed at Young Robert, now standing behind Charlie on the stairs. "Tell cook not to send the usual tray to my room. Ask her to set up a family breakfast in the dining room. We will all eat together."

Lord Chester spoke up. "Ask my valet to send up a bath, too, will you, Robert?"

Nodding, the footman departed, and Lord Chester turned to go.

"All of us," the countess told him firmly.

"Yes, ma'am. *After* a nice, hot bath." The earl winked at

Julia, saluted Charlie and headed back to his rooms, on the other side of the house.

Julia's head dropped.

"I'll bring your things to the blue room, Miss," Susan said as everyone else began to drift away.

"Thank you." She moved closer to the lady's maid and lowered her tone. "And please tell Charlie it was a lovely thought."

Susan gave a small shake of her head. "He'll feel that much worse if he thought you knew it was him."

"Oh." Surprised, Julia frowned—and then she glanced down toward the corridor where the earl had disappeared. She could feel the flush rising. "Oh."

Susan bit back a grin. "I'll meet you in the blue room, Miss."

CHESTER TOOK up a plate at the buffet set up in the dining room, but turned as Miss Deering entered.

She met his gaze and blushed crimson, though not as brilliantly as she'd done earlier.

"Good morning," he said cheerfully. "Shall I fix you a plate?" She looked as neat as a pin in a navy gown that was far sleeker than the disheveled robe he'd seen her in this morning. Her eyes looked clearer, but her face glowed pink in the morning light.

"Yes. Thank you," she told him.

"You sound better," Grandmama said. "Less congested."

"Yes, Cook had me hovering over a bowl of hot water and camphor. It cleared my head wonderfully."

"Well, it wouldn't have been much trouble, as she was already heating water."

He shot his grandmother a quelling look as he set a plate

in front of her companion. Miss Deering was stumbling into another apology. And he was trying not to stare at the way her gown hugged her generous curves. Or wonder if he could bring about such a flushed and dewy look with a kiss, or a run of his hands over those . . .

No. He meant to change. He might begin the transformation by not mentally seducing the woman he'd hoped would help.

"No, no," his grandmother told her. "It's over now. The less said, the better. Now, as for you, Chester . . ." She scraped up the last of her porridge and pointed the spoon at him. "Have you made a decision about your theatrical performance?"

"Ah, no. I'm at a loss."

"Best get on with it. You'll want time to prepare." She tilted her head as she looked at him. "Why not do a song or something you recall from your earlier Christmas celebrations? You said you were pining for a Christmas like those days of old."

His jaw tightened. "Arranging a happy Christmas is one thing, but maudlin reminiscence is another. You know how I feel about dredging up the past." He shrugged. "In any case, perhaps I should withdraw. I'm not sure performance is one of my skills."

She raised her brows at him. "You are going onstage. If I have to, so do you. And in any case, the servants are looking forward to it."

"I wonder if it isn't a case of being too familiar with them. Mightn't it upset the order of things?"

His grandmother set down her napkin. "I had the same thought, the first year we attempted it, but it appears to have had the opposite effect. All of the staff adore the show and in truth, they seem generally happier and more satisfied than ever."

Chester wondered if that was due to the Christmas theatrical—or perhaps to the soothing presence of Miss Deering among them, all year long.

"And it was all your idea?" Charlie said to Miss Deering around a mouthful of bacon. "See? Lord Chester was right. You are thoughtful."

"Yes. Listen to the boy," Chester said with a grin. "That was an observation, not a false assumption."

His grandmother frowned. "Have you been making assumptions, Chester? About Miss Deering?"

"Don't look at me like that, Grandmama. It was only a small one. How could anyone have supposed that she'd only ever received one present?"

"One present?" Charlie asked. "Ever?"

"No," she corrected gently. "One present, before I came to Moreland." She smiled at the dowager. "And a multitude of good fortune, since I arrived."

"What was the one present?" the boy persisted.

She hesitated.

"Tell us," the dowager countess said. "If you've a mind to, that is."

"Lord Chester has said he's not fond of dredging up the past."

Chester met her gaze. He wanted to hear. He suddenly wanted to know all the secrets those gold-flecked brown eyes hid away. "It's my own pain and misdeeds I don't care to revisit." He shrugged. "You may delve into your own as you like."

"Please?" asked Charlie.

She heaved a great sigh. "Very well. I'm sorry to say, Charlie, that it was a dress."

The boy did look disappointed.

"I'm sure it was very beautiful," his grandmother asserted. "A girl is always happy to get a pretty dress."

"It was not," Miss Deering said. "And I had so hoped it would be."

"Who gave you an ugly dress?" Charlie asked.

"My father did. You see, I'd been invited to a party—my first. It was a birthday celebration for one of the young men that my father taught. I knew him well, as he was always at the house for extra lessons. He needed them," she said with a little laugh. "But he was a very nice young man and we had great talks about history. He never minded listening to me go on about Queen Elizabeth."

"A strong, intelligent and savvy woman," said the dowager countess. "Though it was a shame none of it could bring her happiness, along with power."

"We're talking about Miss Deering right now, Grandmama," Chester told her. "And her young man."

And he was not growing irritable at the thought of her, starry-eyed with youthful infatuation and trading intellectual tidbits with her first love.

No, he told himself firmly. *He was not.*

"Oh, he wasn't my young man, but we were friends. He invited me to his party, along with other young people my age. There was going to be dancing. My first chance to dance. I desperately wanted to go, but I didn't have anything suitable to wear. I asked my father if I might get a new dress and he made encouraging sounds, but he was deep in the midst of deciphering an old Saxon document and I knew he wouldn't be any good to me or anyone else until he finished. I figured I'd missed my chance, but the morning of the party, a box arrived."

"He'd heard you, after all?" Charlie asked.

"He had. I'm not sure where he ordered the dress from, but I was so excited—until I opened it. I know that makes me sound horridly ungrateful."

"If I was a girl, I wouldn't want to wear an ugly dress," Charlie said loyally.

"It wasn't ugly, exactly. The quality was good. It was of a brocaded sarsnet, which sounds lovely, but in reality, it was a very plain, dull brown color, not flattering at all, with a square cut neck and no trim."

"Good heavens." His grandmother looked as indignant as Chester felt.

"Fashion was not your father's strong suit, then?" he said gently.

She laughed. "No. I don't think he ever noticed what anyone wore, including himself. He was pleased enough with it, as he said it matched my eyes."

"No one should ever equate your eyes with a dull, brown, plain gown," Chester objected.

His grandmother glanced his way, brow raised, but he ignored her.

Miss Deering looked down at her plate. "That's very kind of you, sir."

"What did you do?" demanded Charlie.

"I wore it. I endured the snickers of the girls and the pitying glances of the boys. I sat in the corner while the dancing went on and had a rousing debate on which of the Tudor wives endured the most with the young man who had invited me. I gathered my courage and approached the girl who wore the prettiest dress there. It was of the lightest, whitest muslin—all the rage—with the most beautiful, embroidered hem. I asked her who made her gown."

"Did she tell you?" the dowager countess demanded. "Or did she snub you?"

"She told me. And she told all the other girls she doubted I could afford to buy anything from the modiste."

His grandmother nodded and heaved a sigh.

"She was right, but I went to the shop and offered to pay the woman to teach me to embroider. She refused at first, but I showed her the dress and told her my story and finally, she relented. She gave me lessons and I practiced and practiced. And at last, when I felt I had enough skill, I consulted her on color and design, and I embroidered a lovely border of marigolds and dahlias in vibrant autumn colors along the bodice and hem of that brown gown and a shower of falling petals to the skirts. I added a bit of lace at the neckline as well."

"And?" his grandmother demanded.

"It greatly improved the gown. Enough so that I wore it for a couple more years, until I grew too tall, and no one ever pitied me for it again. And—I never stopped embroidering," she said with a little laugh.

Chester stared at her, his chest tightening as he imagined it all. Her hopes, her disappointment, a social disaster—and the bravery and tenacity with which she answered it. She took a blow and turned it into a triumph—and a useful skill. She made him feel ashamed. What had he done with his disappointments, except run from them?

His grandmother was watching her with approval, as well. "Thank you for sharing that story, my dear."

Miss Deering flushed. "Of course."

The dowager countess turned to Charlie. "You see what an example she sets us, don't you, boy? She has inspired me. I think, perhaps, that she has given me an idea." She narrowed her eyes a moment. "I believe I might change my performance for the theatrical, in fact." She stood. "Now, what will the three of you do today, to further your Christmas spirit?"

Standing, Chester pushed away his feelings of inadequacy. That was one skill he'd finely developed. "The wind is still blowing out there and the air is frigid. And so, I've arranged a special morning in the kitchen."

"Would you care to join us, Lady Chester?" Miss Deering asked.

"No. I think I shall be very busy, plotting out my new performance idea. But if you are to make something sweet, you may bring me a sample when you are done."

"It's a bargain, Grandmama." He helped her from her chair. "We shall come up with a tray, presently."

CHAPTER 8

"Thank you for indulging us, Mrs. Jensen." Julia gave a grateful smile. "I know you must be busy."

She kept her attention on the cook in a vain attempt to keep control of her jumping, dancing insides. How was she supposed to act cool and calm when that vision of the earl striding down the corridor, in so much bare, muscled glory, hovered foremost in her mind? She'd barely choked down a bite of breakfast. She'd gladly shared the story of her brown dress—a tale that she'd never shared with anyone—just so she could fix her eyes on Charlie, and away from the earl, as she told it.

"We are in a bit of a frenzy," Mrs. Jensen admitted. "What with our regular duties, the holiday preparations and the wassail party tomorrow. But I don't mind giving up a bit of space, as long as you make enough biscuits to serve the guests."

"We are happy to do our part." The earl carried another bowl of prepared dough to the end of the long, wooden table, where they'd all been relegated. "You will like this, Miss Deering, seeing as you are a fan of Queen Elizabeth's."

Oh, dear. He was big. Hard. Sculpted like a Viking warrior of old—and he *listened*? It was no wonder he'd been the one to finally awake the feminine side of her nature. He was a huge, smiling, irreverent, commanding mountain of a man and after years of slumber, her female fancies were urging her to climb him and stake her claim.

Lord Chester whipped the cover off of a bowl. "We are to make gingerbread figures—and perhaps you did not know, but the first ones were designed by Good Queen Bess. She had her kitchens make figures to resemble the dignitaries in her court and served them up at dinner."

"Did she? I had no idea. But I admit, I am an admirer. She had the strength to survive so many webs of intrigue, both personal and political. Her long rule resulted in peace and stability for England." And she served as a fine example of resisting inconvenient desires, she told herself sternly.

Julia smiled over at Charlie. "I like to choose strong women for my pieces in the Christmas theatrical. Last year I was Queen Elizabeth. Although, I confess, one of the reasons was that I wanted to see what it was like to wear one of those large ruffs around my neck."

Charlie nodded, but he was occupied with copying Mrs. Jensen as she showed him how to roll the dough out to the correct thickness. "In some other places, they use a mold to make the figures, but we're going to cut ours out ourselves," she told him.

"Like this." Lord Chester had already cut his first. He peeled it up and set it on a baking tray. "*Et voila!*"

They all peered at it.

"Oh! How talented you are!" Julia gasped. It was clearly Queen Elizabeth, complete with a ruff.

Charlie's eyes widened. "I'll never manage anything like that." He gazed doubtfully at his expanse of dough. "What shall I try?"

"A nativity scene?" the earl suggested.

He made a face. "I would feel strange biting into them. They are *holy*,"

he said seriously.

"Hmm. I see your point."

"Perhaps the animals, gathered around the manger?" Julia offered.

The boy considered. "Yes. I could manage that, I think."

He set to work, producing a credible sheep and a cow. Julia managed an identifiable chicken. It was pleasant and warm, with the smell of ginger and cinnamon in the air and the noisy bustle of Mrs. Jensen and Ruby, the kitchen maid, getting on with their work, and Young Robert coming and going.

"Here you are." Lord Chester laid a camel-shaped biscuit next to theirs on the tray. "This one surely arrived with the three wise men."

"Maybe we need two more," Charlie said. "And a donkey. You know, like the one that carried Mary?"

There was a noticeable dip in the chatter and clatter around them.

Oblivious, Charlie set to work. "They have long ears, right? And a skinny tail?" He frowned, concentrating. "There was a donkey here at Moreland for a time, wasn't there? I heard the grooms talking about him. Old Henry. It's a strange name for a donkey." He looked up. "Does anyone know why he was named Old Henry?"

No one spoke. Julia saw Ruby and Young Robert exchange glances. Mrs. Jensen looked back at the earl from her stove.

The earl did not look up as he answered. "Perhaps because he was miserable and loud, quite like Henry the Eighth, father of Queen Elizabeth."

"Miserable?" Charlie sounded puzzled. "But he had a

home here. Food and water and shelter. Why would a donkey be miserable?"

It seemed as if everyone in the kitchen was holding their breath, waiting on the earl's answer.

Lord Chester's lips pursed. He looked as if he did not wish to answer at all. "He was lonely," he said at last.

"Oh." Charlie grew quiet. "I didn't realize animals get lonely, too."

"Don't despair," Ruby said desperately. "Old Henry cheered up, eventually."

Charlie looked around the kitchen. "How?"

Silence.

"He found a friend," the earl said firmly. "Now, what will you make next? A Christmas star, perhaps?"

"Oh. Yes. I can manage that."

"And in Queen Elizabeth's grand tradition . . ." The earl presented a biscuit with a flourish. "What do you think?"

Charlie stared. "It's Mrs. Jensen! I can see her apron and she's holding a spoon!"

"Now, Lord Chester," the cook admonished. But Julia noted the flush of pleasure in her cheeks.

"Who should we do next?" the earl asked.

"Let's make a likeness of Grandmother," the boy said eagerly.

"Hmm . . . perhaps I can depict her bent at her desk, with a quill."

The regular noise of the kitchen resumed. Julia concentrated on her task, but her mind was busy. The tension in the room had been clear. It was obvious Lord Chester *truly* did not like to revisit the past. He was avoiding something—more than one something, if she had to guess. She frowned. If he truly wanted to change . . . it likely wasn't a good idea.

She was sliding her collection of stars, mangers and a

couple of angels onto the next tray when the earl slid his latest next to hers, with a flourish.

"For you."

She smiled. "Thank you." It was Boudicca, her hair wild and her sword arm raised.

"You must have her for your tea. I made only one, as she is one of a kind—just as you are."

He stood so near. Her skin tingled as she looked up at him. He searched her face, as if looking for her reaction, and he smiled, his shoulders dropping a little, as he found it.

She had to stop herself from leaning toward him. Such a conundrum of a man. Handsome, strong, kind, giving—and holding tightly to some very wrong notions.

A true friend would point it out, try to guide him past such harmful deflections. But she'd seen his stubbornness— and now, how wary others were of it. Advice, no matter how sound, would not be well received, she suspected. Did she want to risk it?

Blinking, she looked away from that sapphire gaze. Charlie was hovering with Mrs. Jensen as she pulled a tray from the ovens.

"The first batch is already cooled, Miss. Would you mind carrying a tray with a pot of tea up to her ladyship?"

"Not at all. We promised her a sample."

Ruby placed a plate of biscuits on a tray and transferred a teapot onto it, as well.

"Here, I'll carry it up for you." The earl looked to Charlie. "Are you coming up with us?"

"No, sir."

"Charlie has promised to help with the last bit of dough," Mrs. Jensen said. "I'll send him up as soon as we finish."

Julia nodded. Her head awhirl and her gut still conflicted, she followed the earl out. She was shallow enough to let the sight of his broad back and strong legs soothe her as they headed upstairs."

CHESTER PAUSED JUST inside the threshold of his grandmother's sitting room. She was not seated as usual, attending to her correspondence. Instead, she hovered over the desk, thumbing through two open volumes and a pile of letters, muttering to herself and going back and forth between them all. As he watched, she turned and reached for another volume from the mantel over the fire.

"Here you are, Grandmama." He set the tray down on a small table. "Won't you come and have a cup of tea? And you must be the judge of our culinary efforts."

"Hmm? No, thank you. Not just yet. I have a lot yet to do, if I am to change my piece for the theatrical." She peered past him. "Ah, do come in, Julia, dear. Your talk of strong women has lit a fire beneath me. We must hold them up. We must strive to follow in their path and encourage others to do so, as well."

"With the *Lattimere Legends*?" Chester asked. He'd read them, years ago. They were witty, amusing, and racy. "Pray do recall, Charlie will be watching. Your selection must be suitable for his tender ears."

"That's just it. I hope it will be exactly what he should hear." The look she gave him was both fond and searching. She beckoned him and he crossed to her. She gripped his arm. "You've influenced me, as well, dear boy."

He squeezed her hand.

"I've no wish to become tangled in the trap that has snared you."

His pleasure ebbed. "Trap?"

"Yes. You sidestep, dance and practically tumble through

your life, trying to ignore your past. I begin to fear it will blight your future."

Chester stilled. Her words were a blow. She'd hinted at it in the past, but this was the first time she'd stated her feelings directly. Still, he was well-armored against such strikes. He could not be angry with her. She cared for him. But she did not understand.

He squeezed her hand again. "We'll have to disagree, Grandmama. But I thank you for your concern."

The thought struck him, then, out of the blue. He wanted to change. Needed to change, as he understood more every day. But not *this*, surely? Not the bedrock upon which he'd built his adult life?

His grandmother stared up into his face for a moment, then heaved a sigh. "We'll speak of it again, sometime." Letting him go, she looked past him again. "I will need your help, my dear. I've set Susan to repairing an old wig. I need you to go up to the attics. In the trunks there is stored the wardrobe of my youth. I need you to find me an old favorite gown."

Miss Deering nodded. "Of course."

"It is a *robe l'anglaise* of green brocade, along with an ivory underskirt and a stomacher embroidered with pink and ivory roses."

"It sounds lovely. I'll go and look now."

"Thank you, dear."

Chester still stood near the desk. He saw the uncertain look Julia Deering sent him as she left. He felt the echo of it in his soul. His grandmother had turned back to her work, so he turned to go and wandered into the passage. He stood a moment, then headed for the servant's stairs. On the landing that separated the stairs to the two separate attics, he listened.

There. Faint footsteps and scrapings led him into the east

attic. Sunlight flooded in, illuminating the appealing sight of Miss Deering's backside thrust high as she burrowed inside a deep trunk. He took a seat on a nearby stool. Its wobble explained its banished status. He contemplated the view, although, truthfully, part of his mind was too occupied to enjoy it.

She dug about for several minutes, lifting the occasional heavy gown aside, but eventually she made a sound of triumph. Standing, she pulled the old-fashioned gown out with her. She let it unfold and held it draped up against her, twisting a bit to set the skirts swishing.

"That green would look lovely on you, but I daresay it would take some time to become accustomed to those wide skirts."

She started and gasped and spun around. "Good heavens! I did not hear you come in."

He nodded.

Folding the gown, she knelt down next to the trunk and began to root about again. After pulling out a couple of more pieces, she closed the lid. Setting the pile of clothing on top, she perched beside it.

They sat there, in the quiet, watching each other for several long moments. Sun shone in, tracing rivers of lighter strands in her hair and dancing with dust motes in the air around her. He watched the spectacle. It helped keep his mind empty.

"Are you all right, my lord?"

He blinked. Sighed. "No."

She waited.

"It's been quite an interesting morning."

She blushed. "I am sorry—"

"No." He cut her off. Snorted. "Honestly, it was nothing. My dog, more than once, coated me with bigger sneezes—"

He froze, biting off the rest of what he'd almost said,

appalled at himself and at where his mind had gone. That was what this morning was doing to him—steering him into places he always deliberately avoided.

Another silence stretched between them.

She frowned, now. She looked as if she were struggling with something. He knew how she felt.

At last, she bowed her head a moment and heaved a sigh. He watched, curious, as she looked up and met his gaze, direct and lifted her chin. "Are you worried, perhaps, sir?"

"Worried?"

"That Lady Chester might be right."

"No." Denial came, instinctive and immediate, even though it was exactly what he'd been thinking. He stood. Paced a bit. Back and forth across the attic. "No. There is no use going back to revisit pain and betrayal."

"Are you sure?"

"What good could it do?" He crossed to stand before her, and she rose to meet him. Her dark eyes had gone wide and her breathing came fast and shallow.

"Perhaps it could bring relief—"

"No. You cannot change what's happened in the past. Better to leave it behind. Better to focus on the present. Give your attention to what is here." He rand his hands along her arms and up to her shoulders. "And now." Pulling her close, he trailed the fingers of one hand up her nape and cupped her jaw.

Her eyes closed. She leaned her face into his hand.

Leaning down—not too far, just the exact right, comfortable amount—he kissed her.

CHAPTER 9

She knew better, but she was weak. Weak in the knees, at the incredible warmth of being folded into his embrace. He towered over and around her, emanating strength and lovely heat.

She was weak with longing, too. His lips were soft. Generous. They gave pleasure, but demanded it as well. Demanded response—and she helplessly answered. She kissed him back, gloried in the sweetness, the surrender, the illusion of safety and belonging.

Illusion.

The truth of it might as well have been a splash of cold water.

She stilled in his arms. Stepped away.

They stared at each other once more. He looked as dazed as she felt.

He swallowed. "I didn't mean . . . That was—"

"Lovely. It was lovely." She steeled her spine. "But it was also a distraction."

He started to protest.

She stopped him with a sharp look. "Is this how you treat your friends, Lord Chester?"

He closed his mouth.

"You asked, but of course you are under no obligation to make me your friend." She stepped away. "However, you will not make me a diversion."

He sank down onto her spot on the trunk. "You are right. Utterly correct." He scrubbed his hand wildly through his hair, then covered his eyes. After a moment, he dropped them and looked up at her. "The thing is, I do wish to be your friend."

His lovely, chestnut hair stood all awry. She felt a visceral need to put her fingers in and smooth it back into order. She tucked her hands behind her back. "Why?"

"Why?"

"There is nothing special about me. Why do you wish to be my friend?"

"Nothing special?" He looked dumbfounded. "Don't be daft."

"I am merely being honest, sir. And I'm asking the same of you."

"And so I shall be. Not special," he scoffed. Pointing a finger at her, he spoke sternly. "You are talented, lovely, kind and useful. Everything I am not." His hand dropped. "And that's the rub, isn't it?"

Julia struggled to breathe normally. He spoke casually, letting devastating compliments roll of his tongue like they were nothing. A shiver ran through her. They weren't nothing. She felt exposed. Seen. And even more dangerous —appreciated.

He looked up. "I think in some ways we are alike."

"Are we?"

"You lost your father a few years ago?"

"Yes."

"And it ripped your world apart? Changed *everything*?"

"Yes," she whispered.

"I was younger, but it was the same for me. You seemed to handle the loss far better than I did. I think, I hope I can learn from you. I wish I had half of your . . . peace and generosity."

"That's why you wish to be my friend?"

"It's part of the reason. There are others." He stood. "But I am also discovering ever more reasons why I wish to kiss you."

Her gaze flew to his mouth, but she stepped backwards. "I think we should stick to friendship. Like false assumptions, I've had too many false kisses to welcome more."

"*False* kisses? Is there such a thing?"

"Assuredly, there is. And I believe you wield them like weapons." Her head lifted. "You've only just done it to me. You only wanted to distract me."

"Perhaps not *only*," he demurred, but he nodded and turned to walk toward the window. He gazed down a moment before turning back. "Will you help me?"

"If I can."

"Will you tell me about your father?"

She stilled. "I told you a bit about him this morning."

"Yes, but I want to know more. How you felt about him and got on with him. What happened when he died and how you ended up here."

She folded her arms in front of her. "Am I to bare my soul while you keep yours shuttered? Friendship must travel two ways, my lord."

His eyes narrowed. "And so we come full circle. There's no point—"

"Yes, yes. No point in revisiting your pain. Why then, must we revisit mine?"

"I . . ." He blinked and his expression fell. "I never thought

. . ." Closing his eyes, he forged ahead. "Since I arrived back at Moreland, I keep discovering new ways in which my behavior has affected others' lives. I want . . . I need to do better." He let out a long sigh. "I want to understand."

For a moment, she considered going along. Giving him what he wanted instead of what she truly believed he needed. It would be easier. It would stand a greater chance of preserving whatever friendliness might survive between them. But it would not be the act of someone who truly wished him well.

Instead, she breathed deeply. "I know you disagree, but if you wish to compare your reactions to mine, it will still require you to examine the events and behaviors in your own past. How else can you think to change your future choices?"

He blew out a huff of air. "You are all relentless, aren't you? Fine. I give in." He scowled. "Did you think I didn't feel the tension in the kitchen this morning? Notice your curiosity? Very well. I'll tell you that tale—and you can disapprove of me as thoroughly as everyone else."

That sounded ominous. But Julia merely perched on his abandoned stool and waited.

"Fine, then." He didn't look at her, but returned to the window. "As I said, my father's passing was difficult for me. The complications that followed only made me feel worse. I began to spend more time here, rather than at home in Devonshire. It helped, but still, I was plagued with worries, fears, resentments. Then one morning, Grandmama called me up to her sitting room. She gave me a basket and said it contained a friend. A companion. A confidante. A responsibility. She warned me I must take it all seriously."

He paused, clearly caught up in a memory. She waited quietly. And then he turned to look at her and smiled.

"It was a mastiff pup, with a brindled coat, a black mask

and a puff of white on his chest. It was love at first sight. I named him Ensign, as I'd recently been enamored of a naval story, in which an ensign performed heroic feats." He sighed. "He made things better. We were devoted to each other. I don't think that dog left my side for the better part of two years. When it came time to go to school, I refused to leave him. I nearly ended up taught at home with tutors, but in the end, Grandmama arranged rental of a private house where I could take Ensign with me. And when I eventually made friends at school—good friends—the only family I have, beyond Grandmama and Charlie—they moved in as well." A smile lit up his whole face. "And didn't we have grand times?"

"It happened when I came back here for a summer leave. We heard it as we approached the house, a caterwauling coming from the stables. Grandmama was frazzled. She'd taken a donkey as a barter payment from a tenant at one of her estates and had him brought here, thinking to use him at the apple press. But the animal was . . . unhappy. No one knew if it was the move or some unseen condition, but the animal was mean and temperamental. Inconsolable. Nor was he shy about expressing his misery, loudly and continuously.

"I went to take a look at him. Old Starkie had reached his limit. He wanted to send him to the knackers, but . . ."

His words trailed away. Julia was bursting with curiosity. "What happened?"

"Ensign walked up to that braying beast and stood nose to nose with him. It was eerie, almost as if they were communicating. And Old Henry stopped squalling."

"Oh, dear."

"He was a different animal, docile, content. He would frolic a bit, when sent out to pasture—but only when Ensign was with him."

"Oh, no."

"Oh, yes. I fought it, at first. I would take Ensign with me into the village or try to keep him with me at night. But Old Henry would start up again. No one was sleeping and Ensign would just stand at the door, patiently waiting for me to let him out."

"That must have been heartbreaking for you."

"It was. Of course, Ensign and I still cared for each other, but Old Henry needed him. I knew it, but still, I was furious. I hated that damned donkey. I resented Grandmama for bringing him here, and Ensign for abandoning me. Hell, I resented the whole damned world. I was a bigger, more sullen ass than Old Henry."

Julia bit back a smile. She could imagine the pain he must have suffered.

"I returned to school without my best friend, and I stayed away. I barely returned to Moreland for the next couple of years. Old Henry and Ensign, meanwhile, had the run of the place. Ensign was big and smart and could open nearly any gate. They used to amble about the orchards and the woods and make occasional forays into the neighbor's cabbage patch. I found other ways to console myself and kept away—until Grandmama wrote to tell me that Old Henry had died."

"What did you do?"

"I came back to fetch Ensign. He was old and greying by then. I spent a summer taking him on adventures. We did all of his favorite things. We ate beefsteak and slopped through puddles and I let him chase squirrels in the park. We went to my friend Whiddon's hunting box and took long walks in the woods. We went to Weymouth and explored the seashore. It was like old times for a couple of months, then he passed on, too."

She silently contemplated the whole tale, imagining it all. But then she frowned. "Wait. I understand that it might be painful, going over such memories. But why did you say that I would despise you?"

"Why wouldn't you?"

"I'm afraid you'll have to explain."

"Explain what?" He sounded exasperated.

"Just what was so despicable about your behavior in that story?"

"Weren't you listening? I acted a sullen, resentful child."

"Ah." She nodded. "In reality, you were a child, or at least a very young man."

"That doesn't excuse the neglect. I stayed away from Grandmama, the one person who had done so much for me. Not to mention, I might have visited Ensign, at least."

"Yes, I can see where that would weigh on you. I'm sure Lady Chester did miss you. She cares for you deeply, you know?"

"I do know. And I care for her. I'm only just realizing how much—and how much I have missed."

"But I also imagine it would have been a fresh loss for you, every time you came and left without your companion."

"Yes, but I let it become a habit, staying away. I didn't return, even later. That horrible tale is not the whole reason, I admit. It's not even close to the worst story I could tell you."

"We all have made mistakes. We all have regrets. But in my opinion, this story is not half as bad as it has grown in your mind."

He shook his head.

"Let me tell what I heard. I heard a story of giving. You and Ensign both gave up your steady, loyal, comfortable companionship to ease another creature's suffering. And don't tell me it doesn't matter because the creature was just a donkey."

"It's not as if I had a choice," he argued.

"Of course, you did. You all did. You could have forced Ensign to leave with you. Lady Chester could have sent Old Henry to the glue yard. It sounds to me like Ensign had a calling and you sacrificed your own comfort to allow him to follow it. And though it felt like he abandoned you, when it was over, you came back and made sure his last months were filled with love and joy." She sighed. "It is a sad story, to be sure, but I think it has grown worse, pushed away in some hidden corner of your heart."

Frowning, he turned back toward the window.

"You know, I've known some people who hold onto pain and resentment. They let it prick and drive them, but it rarely does any good, and in the end, it only makes them miserable."

He stiffened, but she continued. "You say it is better to avoid and ignore the pain in your past, and yet it feels like the same thing is happening to you."

She'd gone too far. He stood poker straight and his breath had begun to come quickly. She tried again. "Don't you feel a little better, after talking about it?"

He pushed away from the window and strode toward her. Her stomach lurched a little, in surprise and in nervous fascination at the odd look on his face. He marched up to her and grabbed her shoulders pulled her to a standing position. "I feel better looking at it through your eyes. Your lovely, luminous eyes that see the best in all around you." He searched her face. "You meant it, didn't you?"

She nodded as her heart rate ratcheted.

He let her go and turned away. But he looked back over his shoulder, as if he couldn't help it. "Damn it," he cursed.

It startled her. She had gone too far, perhaps.

He pivoted and suddenly he was before her again, and his hands were cupping her jaw. "I want you to know, I *mean* this."

He kissed her.

Again.

Oh, but this was not the same. This kiss was not a tactic,

nor a weapon. It was . . . sweetness. Light. His lips moved softly over hers. She savored the feel and taste of him and gripped him suddenly, when he shifted and slid his tongue into her mouth.

This was it, then. Her first real kiss. The sort she had craved. One that spoke of closeness and harmony. One that said *Hello* and *Welcome* and *Look what we can do together.*

She gave herself over to it. She pressed into him and he slid his arms around to her back. Warmth again. And glorious safety. And this time, it felt real.

His lips were soft, but the rest of him felt hard. She sent tentative fingers over his shoulders, felt the muscles contained by the layers of his clothes. She let her fingers drift higher, up and along his neck and into his disheveled hair.

She dug her fingers in and messed it up further.

A door slammed, not so very far away.

They froze.

Footsteps sounded on stairs.

Their lips parted.

"Miss Deering? Did you find that gown?"

"Susan," she whispered. They broke apart.

"Miss Deering?"

"Yes, Susan. I found the right gown," she called. She stepped over to the trunk and took up the bundle of clothes. Placing her finger against her lips, she stared at him a moment, then headed for the stairs. "I found all the pieces of the outfit, too." She headed down the stairs. "There are a great many lovely things up here, but this meets the description, I believe."

She'd caught Susan on the way up. The maid looked her over, but made no comment, just headed back down.

Julia followed, looking over her shoulder, but there was no sight or sound of Lord Chester.

~

CHARLIE LEFT THE KITCHENS, feeling thoughtful. Making biscuits had been fun and cook had agreed to help him with some special ones, after Chester and Miss Deering left the kitchen. Together, they'd managed to craft the silhouettes of a gentleman and a lady. At first, he'd hoped to have them hold hands, but it proved problematic. Mrs. Jensen had suggested they each hold a glass and they could be joined together to clink glasses in a toast.

"It's appropriate enough, as the earl does enjoy his cup of cheer," she said.

They had turned out well. Two of each. He hoped to sneak a pair into both Chester's and Miss Deering's rooms while the party kept them busy, tomorrow evening. Nick had suggested he do something to put the idea into their heads, and Charlie thought it was a nice way to do it.

Truthfully, though, he felt he must face the notion that his plan might not work. The chestnuts and the greenery had been disasters. And the pair of them were still looking at each other, but going no further, that he could tell.

Disappointment washed over him. The three of them got on so well. They could laugh together. They could look past mistakes—like the fir amongst the greenery. They would make a fine family. He sighed. He did long to be part of a family again. To belong. To care and be cared for.

He supposed he would still have some of it, with Chester, after the holidays. For the amount of time it took for them to find him a school or a tutor who took boarders. They would stay together while they searched, at least. And afterwards, he would stay in touch with the earl. Chester would agree, if Charlie asked. He would keep his word.

A family would be so much better.

And that would leave Miss Deering alone. Mostly alone.

She would have grandmother, who was a grand old lady, but she kept to her rooms most of the time.

Charlie recalled the earl's words this morning—about Old Henry. Mrs. Jensen had whispered the story in his ear, while they worked on the special biscuits.

Old Henry had found a friend. That's what Chester had said. If Charlie and the earl left without her, perhaps Miss Deering might need a friend.

He had an idea about that. But how to go about it?

Fetching his coat and his hat, he set out for the village. Perhaps Nick would know.

CHAPTER 10

Chester sat for a while, alone, in the quiet of the attic. He tried to blank his mind, but it wouldn't cooperate. Eventually, he went down to fetch his coat and strode out to the stables, where he had Old Starkie set the lads to removing all of the fir from the greenery in the tack room. He looked for Charlie, but the lad was nowhere to be found, so he went out alone to fetch replacements for the fir.

Just as well the boy was somewhere else. His thoughts just wouldn't cooperate. That kiss. Heaven help him, he had meant it. In a way that he never had before, in his life. He kept reliving it—and then his head would whirl off with the echo of Julia Deering's words.

Had she been right? In pushing his misdeeds into some dark corner of his soul, had he allowed them to grow more monstrous than they needed to be?

He spent a while doing what he never did—reexamining his own worst moments. He found that in some cases her wisdom held, but in others . . .

She couldn't have known how closely her words would strike—those about holding onto pain and resentment. He already knew, in intimate detail, how miserable that could make a person—and everyone around them, too.

But the idea that running from pain, avoiding or ignoring it, could lead to the same end?

The thought shook him to his core.

It was late afternoon before he returned to Moreland and dropped off the fresh greenery. The stable lads had recruited Ruby and a couple of the maids to help. They looked a cheerful bunch as they worked and laughed and sang the songs of the season. It was too much merriment for his current mood. He found himself missing his friends. They understood his need to be moving ever forward.

Standing outside in the growing dark, he watched the house. What was Julia Deering doing now? Likely, she was frantically busy with preparations for the next days of festivities.

He should offer assistance. But she would look at him with those seeing eyes and he didn't trust himself not to seek oblivion by clutching her close and kissing her senseless. By letting loose that dark mane of hair and exploring her wealth of curves—

Damn.

He set out for the village. Almost without thinking, he found himself at the cooper's shop. Stepping in, he was overwhelmed with the scent of varnish. "Marc," he said to the man stooped over a worktable.

His childhood friend looked up and a grin spread all over his face. "Your lordship!" Wiping his hands, he set a frame over his project and draped a canvas over it. "Good to see you, Chester!" Crossing over, Marc gave him a cracking embrace and thumped him on the back. "Still brawny as ever, aren't you? I didn't think to see you until the party tomorrow."

"Are you busy? I just thought I'd stop in and see how you are getting on."

"Oh, I'm grand! Would you care to come and meet my Jeannie?"

"I'd love to meet her—but perhaps tomorrow? I was hoping you might go over to the Boar's Head with me."

Marc looked him over. "Like that, is it?"

Chester sighed. "I'm tired of thinking. Let's go drink. And for God's sake, don't let me have any of that apple flavored rotgut."

His friend laughed. "No. That stuff might stop you from thinking permanently." He shrugged into his coat. "Come on, then, old man. Let's go."

THE REST of Julia's day was a whirlwind of preparations. She helped Susan start the refitting of Lady Chester's old gown, and then she and the dowager countess saw to the last preparations of the Boxing Day gifts. She consulted with Mrs. Jensen on the recipe for the wassail for the next day's party and on the plan to place the *hors d'oeuvres* on a buffet table in the dining room. She and Charlie had a grand time practicing their verbal duel as Roman general and Boudicca. She grew a little wistful as they did. Charlie was slowly blooming. He was smart and funny, and he was starting to let it show. She wished they would have more time together. She got her wish, after they finished, as Lady Chester had asked for a tray in her rooms and the earl had not returned, so the pair of them shared dinner in the nursery.

And all through the day, as her mind stayed occupied, her heart had insisted on warbling an ill-advised song. *He kissed me. Chester kissed me. And he meant it.*

Ill-advised, she kept reminding herself, because nothing

more would come of it. He'd been emotional. Perhaps a little grateful. And though it had been a shattering event for her, for him it was just one of hundreds of kisses.

Perhaps thousands, if the stories were true.

It didn't matter. It had been a true kiss. He'd seen her. Heard her. Responded to her, Julia Deering. In that moment she hadn't been an orphan, an object, a girl too tall or too educated or too odd to fit easily, anywhere.

It was a moment she would treasure, always.

She wouldn't waste time or court heartache by wishing for more.

Now, at last, the day was ending, and she had a bit of extra time for herself. She went to her room, thoroughly aired out now, and sighed at the festive sight. Charlie was such a dear, sweet boy. She was going to miss him when he left.

She lit the room brightly and settled down with the embroidery to line Lord Chester's box. The book and bottle were complete. She'd thought to stitch a window in the background, with a winter scene, but a notion had seized her. She could not quite free herself of it. Was she wrong? Would he disapprove? She hoped not. The urge was in her brain, heart and fingers. She set to work, bringing it to fruition.

Time passed and the candles had burned low before she finished. The piece was done. She smoothed it, examining the sweet, brindled, masked face peering in the window. He would remember Ensign fondly, she hoped, whenever he opened his box. And her, too.

Standing, she stretched her back. She blew out the candles, but moonlight shone into the room. She went to the window. The winds had died down. The air was cold and still, and the sky was a blanket of stars. It was a beautiful night, and she had the sudden urge to be out in it.

She didn't question the feeling. It was Yuletide, the time

of magic. She wanted a taste of it. Wrapping up warmly, she went down the servants' stairs, past the kitchens and out the back.

Leaving behind the empty kitchen gardens, the functional courtyard and storage areas, she headed for the low, stone wall that separated the kept grounds from the wood. Perching there, she drank in the beauty of the clear, night sky and the frost-kissed trees.

She hadn't been there long when she heard the servants' door slam. Someone pelted out of the house and skidded on the frosty cobblestones. A curse rang out—and she knew who it was.

She couldn't help herself. He had come out as far as the stacked wood and grabbed a cart.

"What are you doing?" she asked as he began to fill it.

He spun around, holding a split log high. She put her hands up and he relaxed, gaping at her. "What are you doing out here?"

"It was too beautiful to stay inside." She raised a brow. "What is it you are doing?"

"I was drinking with Marc Haskins and I remembered something. Here. Catch." He tossed her a log. "Come on, then. You can help me."

She considered a moment, then she shrugged, tossed the log in the cart and reached for more.

When it was full, Chester grabbed her hand. "Come with me?"

She nodded. He took up the cart handles and pushed, heading in the direction of the stables. He detoured before he got there, however, turning in the direction of the orchards.

"What are we doing?" she asked again.

He pushed the cart into the widest, center-most row. Past the first transverse row of trees sat a stone circle.

"We were talking of the harvest and of the old days, when

we were just ornery boys. I remembered something my grandfather used to do. At Christmas, he would build up a large bonfire here and we would all gather to sing carols. He always sang one song alone, a song to awaken the trees, to inform them of the turn of the seasons, and prepare them for spring. It was meant to increase the harvest in the autumn." He turned to her. "I thought we could bring the party outside to sing to the trees."

She was enchanted. "I think Lady Chester would love that. I'll make sure her wraps are close by and ready." She caught up his hand. "Will you sing your grandfather's song? I think she would be so touched."

He nodded. "I'll have to find someone to help me with the lyrics. Old Starkie might know them."

"Or one of the gardeners."

He nodded. "Let's build up the bonfire and have it all ready. We'll surprise everyone."

They worked together and it was done quickly. Their breath rose like clouds toward the sky.

"Come and sit with me." He'd perched on the end of the cart. "Let's rest a moment, then I'll give you a ride back."

She laughed. "I think I'll walk." But she sat next to him and sighed at the warmth of his leg next to hers.

"The stars never look like this in London." He was gazing up at the sky.

"I'm not sure the stars ever looked like this. They look like diamonds, shining so brightly."

"And still, they are not as lovely as you," he said softly.

He watched her now, intently. "I've been busy most of the day, and my brain has been turning everything over and over at twice its normal speed—and still, there's been a low beat of anger beneath it all, worrying at me."

"Anger?" The chill of the air tried to worm into her heart. She shivered.

"Yes. Two things. I can't rid myself of them."

"What two things?" she whispered.

"False assumptions. And false kisses. It is a crime that you ever had to suffer either."

She ducked her head.

"I know you feel out of step."

"I am." She shrugged. "I always have been."

"As have I, to an extent. Though I admit, a title covers a multitude of sins—and differences."

She snorted.

"Will you tell me? What happened? How you came to Moreland?"

She sighed. "I will, but only because you were generous enough to share a difficult story with me."

"I'll take it," he said with a grin. Taking her hand, he tucked it between his own. "Tell me."

Where to begin? "It's true, though. I've always been out of step, as you put it. I learned domestic matters early, mostly out of necessity. It was just my father and me and a succession of housekeepers, who would leave because Father forgot to pay them or forgot to pay the coal man or the butcher's bill."

He gave a groan.

She lifted a shoulder. "I was always different from other girls my age. My clothes were often too small because I grew fast and Father didn't notice. I knew too much about some things and not enough about others. I was more comfortable around boys because they were always about, coming in for lessons or extra tutoring. They tolerated me, but I was never one of them, nor was I the sort of girl they were used to. But it was all superficial, social troubles—until my father died."

"What happened?"

"My father had been buried only days before the school hired his successor. Our house was one of the advantages to the position. The new professor arrived to inspect the place —and informed me that I might stay on as his housekeeper, as he'd heard I was odd but efficient, with no family or chance at a suitor. For a slightly increased salary, I could also become his mistress."

Chester looked horrified—and furious. "What did you do?"

"I politely declined. He informed me everyone would make the assumption anyway and he impolitely pressed the issue, so I threatened him with a kitchen knife."

She shivered and Chester pressed closer and put his arm around her. She leaned into his heat. It would be easier to talk if she couldn't see his face.

"The man had the audacity to report me to the dean," she continued. "I was summoned to his office, but I wasn't worried. He'd been a friend to my father and his wife had always been kind to me. She'd invited me to tea in their home, actually, after our appointment."

"I'm glad you had someone to go to."

"So was I. Especially when he said he knew I had kept my father organized and productive. I was wasted as a house-keeper. He would hire me as his assistant."

"I'm afraid I see where this is going," Chester growled.

"Yes. I would help him with his research and papers as well as my duties in the bedroom. Of course, I would have to reside in another town, not too far away. Somewhere he could get to for an afternoon of work and pleasure, without alerting his wife."

"No kitchen knives available this time," he said.

"No, but I was not completely without weapons. I knew the school owed my father money. I told him he could pay what was owed, right then, or I would head straight to his home, tell his wife, and take her with me when I reported his behavior to the school's trustees."

"He was wise enough to pay you, I assume."

"Yes. I returned home only long enough to walk in the front door, pick up the portmanteau I'd had ready since the first incident, go out the back and straight to a coaching inn. I hired a private coach to take me to London and I went to Half Moon House."

"Ah. Hestia Wright, champion of women. You *are* a smart girl."

"She took me right in. I stayed there for only a week or so. She's one of your grandmother's correspondents, and Lady Chester had mentioned she might like to hire a companion. Hestia sent me out as soon as the arrangements could be made for an interview."

Chester's lips pressed together. "I would have given a lot to have witnessed that first meeting."

"Oh, it was good. Lady Chester asked me first off what I thought of Wollstonecraft. I told her I thought it was a shame her private life should affect her legacy, when learned men regularly get away with worse."

He laughed. "I know she liked that."

Julia grinned. "We were fast friends before the morning was out." She snuggled in closer. "We get on well together. I adore your grandmother."

CHESTER SIGHED. "SO DO I."

He adored her, too, he was afraid. And that fear—it was a truth he was only beginning to realize. A convenient side effect of always running, always moving forward and never looking back—most people couldn't keep pace.

He had his friends. Whiddon, Sterne, Tensford and Keswick, they knew his secrets as he knew theirs. Their trust in each other was absolute. But everyone else? He outran them all. Because he was afraid. Those who got close gained the ability to hurt you—and when they wielded the power you gave them, it was devastating.

He bit back a laugh. They were a pair. Julia Deering longed to be seen and he despised the very notion.

She shivered once more, and he tossed away every worry about propriety. Who would see them? He pulled her onto his lap. "Come. Let me keep you warm while I thank you."

She was blushing furiously. He couldn't quite see it, but he could hear it in her tone. "For helping with the bonfire? I love the idea."

"For that. And for telling me hard truths when I didn't wish to hear them."

She ducked her head.

"It's very easy, on the other hand, for me to tell you the truth. I don't even have to tell it, honestly. It shines out of you. All I need do is reflect it back so you may see it."

He tightened his grip on her. "You are not out of step." She started to protest, and he stopped her. "You are a step ahead—a *league* ahead. Beyond anyone I've ever met. I'm so sorry you met with such horrid circumstances, but full credit to you for the strength, dignity and resourcefulness you showed, getting out of it. And not only did you emerge on the other side, but you did it with your kindness, generosity and *light* intact. I am so very impressed by you, Julia Deering. I am in awe of you."

Tears brightened her eyes until they rivaled the stars above them. She made an inarticulate sound and then she leaned in and kissed him soundly.

So sweet. The alluring tenderness of it opened an ache inside of him. *No. No. That was wrong.* She kissed him with ardent inexperience, her lips tempting and eager. He tugged her close and deepened their embrace, sweeping his tongue against hers. She poured it all into him. Everything. Gentle heat, closeness, sweet surrender and innocent, bone-shaking desire. She gave of herself freely and it began to *close* the ache inside of him. He'd been running for so long, but he'd carried that hole with him as he went, and now she filled it with peace and passion and generous ardor.

It woke something fierce in him. Need. Hunger. Not for the jaded pleasures and shallow experiences he was used to pursuing, but for her. He dug a hand in her hair and fisted the other into the thickness of her cape and he kissed her harder, relentlessly searching and reaching for more.

Nearby—very close—an owl hooted. She jumped. Startled eyes flew open and she pulled away.

"Oh, dear." Their breath mingled visibly between them. "Did that sound disapproving to you?"

He reached for sanity, for reason—for the strength not to grab her back and kiss her again and again—and ask for more.

"I think it surely must be." Of course, it was. He was shocked at the intensity of his response to her and worried that he was no fit match for her—surely, the rest of the universe must feel the same way.

Lifting her off of him, he steadied her until she found her feet. "It must be growing late. We should head back."

"Tomorrow will be a long and busy day." She didn't sound eager to return to the house.

She declined to be pushed in the cart, so they walked back, and he left it where he'd found it. When they reached the servants' entrance, they both hesitated. He took her hand in his as they turned back for a last, long glimpse of the beautiful night. It was just clasped hands. Surely this much couldn't be so wrong. He kept a hold of her as they finally entered and headed upstairs.

~

FROM INSIDE THE KITCHEN, Charlie watched them pass. He noticed their hands and smiled in joy and relief. He'd come down to check on the special biscuits after a bad dream in which Mr. Roland Graves found and ate them—now he knew the biscuits were safe and his plan might be working, after all. He crept back upstairs, feeling better than he had in a long time.

None of them heard the servants' door open and close again, saw the flare of a match in the cold air or smelled the resulting plume of cheroot smoke.

Charlie was not the only one smiling.

CHAPTER 11

Soon after the next morning dawned, all of Moreland was alive with anticipation. The servants kept making excuses to detour through the front hall, the parlor, and each successive room where Chester stood on a ladder, hanging greenery.

Charlie stood below, directing Chester where to drape, loop or add red bows. The boy handled all the decoration at the ground level. He was all excitement and smiles this morning and it thrilled Chester's heart to see it. He was so much like his father. Chester thought he might stretch out the process of finding the boy's new school, just to give them some more time together.

But that was the future, and this was Christmas Eve. After they'd finished with every strand, garland and bough, they consulted privately and set about adding bunched sprigs of mistletoe in strategic spots throughout the house.

Julia Deering hurried through as they worked, her arms full of festive linens. She smiled at him as she went, and he was suddenly, thoroughly glad he'd made the effort to collect such a large quantity of mistletoe.

She filled his thoughts. He'd asked her to help him change and she had, but in entirely unexpected directions. He'd hoped she could help set him on a new path—and now he desperately wanted her to walk it with him. Was it possible to ask it of her? Was it fair?

It struck him, when he first woke this morning, that she'd been right about him slowing down enough to confront his past. Perhaps he owed it to her to follow her advice before he contemplated asking her to share his life. Was he ready, finally, to address the real darkness he fought to hold at bay? The one that had started him racing in the first place? He looked toward the stairs. He must consult with his grandmother about it.

He was wiring up the last of the mistletoe onto the entry hall chandelier when a knock sounded on the front door. Young Robert hurried to open it—and Chester nearly fell off his ladder.

"Whiddon?"

His friend strode through the door, grinning from ear to ear as Chester scrambled down to greet him. "What are you doing here, man?"

"I got your message about the gifts you wanted sent on. Hope's lavender products were easy enough to come by, but those fancy editions you wanted, they were harder to find. By the time I had everything, I decided I might as well deliver them myself."

"I'm so glad you did. You must stay for Christmas, of course. We should love to have you."

Whiddon glanced around. "You are doing it up in style, aren't you? I thought I would find you holed up in the local tavern. I remember drinking there with you and I thought I recalled a barmaid with—"

His friend blinked and paused as Charlie came to stand at Chester's side. Grinning, Chester set a hand on the boy's shoulder. "Lord Whiddon, may I present my charge, Master Charles Edgerton?"

"Edgerton? Your cousin's boy?" Whiddon's eyes widened. "It's a pleasure to meet you, young sir. Chester always has fond words—and wild tales—to share when he speaks of your father."

Charlie's manners were perfect as he greeted Whiddon and Chester beamed with pride. His friend gave him an odd look. "My man will bring in your packages. Can you put him up as well?"

"Of course. Charlie, run and fetch Mrs. Eckles or Miss Deering, will you?"

"Miss Deering?" Whiddon asked as the boy ran off.

"Grandmama's companion."

"Ah, I didn't know I came to rescue you, but I am glad to do it. Why don't we head out to that tavern? We really must talk."

Chester made a face. "I cannot, I'm afraid." He pulled his friend into the parlor. "We've a wassail party planned for tonight and it's a surprise for Grandmama. I really must stay and help with the preparations."

"Must you?" Whiddon frowned. "Now, don't you start to go domestic on me, too."

"What do you mean?"

"You know what I mean! First Tensford, then Keswick, and Sterne, too. They are falling like toy soldiers."

Chester bit back a grin. "Fallen? I think you mean married."

"What's the difference?"

"I don't think they view Hope, Glory or Penelope as the enemy."

"Well, I might."

"Come on, Whiddon. You've met them. Lovely girls, each

and every one. And last I checked, Tensford, Sterne and Keswick are happier than pigs in swill."

"I know you are right," Whiddon said on a sigh. "But it's not the same."

Chester sobered. "No. It's not. But neither are we. We're not young bucks racketing about Town anymore."

"Well, they are not, but thank all the gods that you and I are. In fact, that's what I've come to talk to you about." He spied the sideboard and went to pour himself a drink. "I've a message from Deliah."

"Deliah?" He paused a moment, waiting to see what he might feel, hearing her name.

Nothing.

"There was a massive row at Thorpe's. Her husband left to spend the holiday with his mistress. His mother has gone off in a huff, bound for the family estate. Deliah sends word that all is clear for you to come to her."

Still nothing. A week he ago he would have jumped at the chance. But looking back, he saw that there had been nothing real in their relationship. It had been all lust and drama and the small, secret hope that *she* might hear of it, and the scandal would irritate her endlessly. His mother.

"I don't think you should go," Whiddon told him.

"You don't?" This was unexpected.

"No. Deliah is not rational at the moment. She's going on about a separation from Knelling, babbling that you will stand by her when all of the world shuns her. She keeps talking about living with you in some love nest, alone forever —as if she would ever forgo the chance to become a marchioness or give up her glittering position in Society."

"No. She may be furious with Knelling now, but she'll never leave him."

"Good man. I'm glad you see it." Whiddon's demeanor brightened considerably. "I tell you what, let's leave. Go.

Now. We can head back to London and go on a real carouse, just you, me, a river of liquor and as many girls as we can find."

Chester smiled fondly at his friend. He might have predicted that change would hit Whiddon the hardest—if he hadn't expected himself to be incapable of it. Yet, here he stood, suddenly recognizing that he'd already left his old path behind and was walking on the new one with eager purpose. "I'm afraid I can't. I've made commitments here. It would break Grandmama's heart if I left."

Nodding, Whiddon capitulated. "She's a treasure, that one. A feisty, sharp-tongued treasure, but there you have it." He downed the rest of his drink. "Well, I'll stay, and we'll plan our decadence for after the holidays."

"I hate to say it, but I'm fairly certain my carousing days are done."

Whiddon scowled. "What are you saying?"

"It had to happen someday. I fear I've stopped running."

Whiddon snorted. "You, Chester?"

"Hard to believe, I know."

Slamming down his glass, Whiddon came closer and searched his face. "Don't tell me. Never say it. There's a woman involved, isn't there?"

He grimaced and shrugged. "I'm not certain, to be honest. But, damnation, I do hope so."

Rubbing his temple, his friend turned away. "Hell, not you, too. This is . . ." He turned back. "Are you sure?"

He nodded. "I am sorry. I know this sort of change upsets you—"

"Me? Hell, no. I'm fine. It's the rest of you who have lost your wits." Whiddon shook his head. "See my man settled, would you? And see to your duties. I'm going to spend my afternoon at that tavern."

"Whiddon—"

His friend strode out and Chester heard the front door slam behind him. He stood a moment, torn. But as much as he hated change, Whiddon was going to have to adapt. He could do it. He was too devoted to his friends to resent their happiness for long.

Look at his own transformation. Chester spent a moment marveling at how quickly everything could change, before realizing that although he felt transformed on the inside, he had steps to take to shape his new reality. Leaving the parlor, he headed upstairs.

He found his grandmother at the window in her sitting room, reading out loud. "Are you practicing for the theatrical?" he asked when she spotted him. "May I interrupt?"

"Of course." She set her book aside and went to the chair before the fire. He saw her settled, moved to take the other chair—and then changed his mind. Folding himself over at her feet, he laid his head in her lap, as he used to do.

She stiffened, but then the tension ebbed out of her and she put her fingers in his hair. He'd always loved it when she did that.

"Whiddon has arrived."

"That rascal?"

"I asked him to stay."

"Of course. You must. That boy needs settling."

The quiet continued a while. "Have you heard from her?" he asked at last.

She knew who he meant. "Yes."

"Should I go to her? Would it help?"

Her fingers stopped. "Oh, my darling boy. She has not changed. She's still bitter and angry. Still blaming you, me, God himself, everyone but herself for her misery. I don't know that it would do any good to see her. I'm not sure you can reach her. I'm not sure anyone can. She's built those grandiose walls of fury and fear high."

He let out a shuddering breath.

"But, my dear boy, I do understand what you've done, how you've grown, just to contemplate such a step."

"I'm trying, Grandmama. I want to do better. By you. By Charlie." He paused. "I want to be worthy."

She reached down and urged him to lift his head. "Does she feel the same way?"

"I think so." His eyes briefly closed. "I hope so."

"She is a fine girl with a big heart and a lovely spirit. You've always been a fine man, Chester. You just had to discover it for yourself." She smiled at him. "In my eyes, you've just proven yourself worthy of her."

"Thank you," he whispered.

"There's magic in this time of year, my boy. Go and make it work for you."

Julia's nerves fluttered as she dressed for the party. Chester had not yet seen her in her best gown, a sage green silk that she thought complemented her skin. She added a new sash of deep maroon. There. She represented the season very well. A pinch of her cheeks and she hurried out for a last-minute check on the preparations.

Oooh. Chester stood in the empty hall at the bottom of the stairs. He looked resplendent in black, formal breeches and coat, with a maroon-colored waistcoat.

She blushed. They would perhaps look like they belonged together.

He heard her step and turned to look up. Their gazes met. She had no recollection of making her way down the stairs. She might have floated. All she knew was that he was waiting for her and took her hand at the bottom. They stared, lost, gazing at each other with pleasure. Who knew how much time passed?

A throat cleared. Chester blinked, then led her to the parlor. "Miss Deering, I'd like to introduce you to one of my dearest friends. Lord Whiddon, may I present Miss Deering?"

Chester's friend possessed fine manners, very formal and perhaps a little curt, but she did not have time to worry over it. Young Robert, positioned to watch the door so no one would knock and alert the dowager countess, admitted the first guests.

They came in streams, then, and Julia and the earl had them keep their wraps and gather in the parlor, as quietly as possible. When the room filled, Chester dispatched Charlie to draw Lady Chester out of her rooms.

She came on the boy's arm, stopping at the railing as she spotted the full hall below. Chester started to sing. Everyone else joined in and the dowager smiled widely from above.

"Thank you, all," she called when they finished. "Welcome!" She grinned at Charlie. "And isn't this a fine bit of Christmas magic?"

The crowd cheered for her and a flurry of well wishes and season's greetings drifted upward. Julia's heart soared at the happiness in the dowager's expression. They'd done it. They'd brought true Christmas spirit to Moreland.

Chester climbed a few stairs and addressed the crowd. "We've another surprise planned, if you will all take a short walk with us, outside."

Julia dashed upstairs, ready with the dowager's outdoor things. She bundled her well, making sure she had a hood, a heavy pair of gloves and a muff for good measure. They made their way outside slowly, following the crowd, which parted to let the dowager through as they came to the orchard.

"Oh," Lady Chester said softly when she spotted the bonfire. "Yes. How lovely." She gripped Julia's hand while everyone sang again, and when Chester stepped forward to sing alone, tears streamed down her face. She held her head high, though, and Julia gave her a handkerchief when it was over.

"It's too cold to stay out here long," she called out. "Now that the trees have been awakened, let's head back inside for wassail and canapés."

She could feel Lady Chester tiring as they headed back. She saw her seated next to the fire, still bundled in an elegant shawl and with a lap blanket. She fetched her a hot drink and a plate of food. Guests moved in, eager to speak with the dowager, and Julia withdrew with a sigh of relief. There. That was all the difficult parts of the evening done. Now she could enjoy herself.

Chester was not in sight, but she spoke with Mrs. Haskins and thanked Mr. Haskins for the delivery of the wooden box this morning. "It's lovely. I have it all lined and ready for Lady Chester to give to his lordship."

"He nearly caught me at it, yesterday," the cooper laughed. "He came in as I was finishing, and I only just got it covered in time."

She told Mrs. Louden how much Charlie loved his Roman helmet and was glad to learn the milliner had commissioned two more similar pieces.

She spoke with several acquaintances from church and finally began to wonder where Chester had got to.

"Mrs. Eckles, have you seen the earl, lately?"

"No, indeed." The housekeeper was poised out of the way near the dining room, where the food was laid out. "I don't think he's eaten at all. Have you, Miss?"

"Not yet."

"Well, I know those apricot pastries are your favorite. Go and grab a plate before everything is gone."

"I will. Will you move into the parlor to keep an eye on Lady Chester, as I do? Fetch me if she needs anything. I'll watch the buffet while I eat."

The housekeeper moved on and Julia took her time filling her plate. Mrs. Jensen had outdone herself. Most of the guests had been through already, but there was still plenty of festive food left—including the cook's famous apple dumplings and good cream to go over them. She moved slowly, taking a bite here and there and filling her plate, and keeping an eye out for the earl.

When she reached the end of the line, she found herself next to the opening of the butler's pantry. Someone was in there. Male voices drifted out. She recognized Chester's tone.

She started forward. Had something gone wrong? But as she drew near, she heard her name. Her nerves started to flutter again.

"I'm telling you, Chester, it's true." It was Lord Whiddon in there with him, and the earl's friend did not sound happy. "I gather you think you feel something for this girl, but you need to reconsider. I believe she's even worse than Deliah."

Who was Deliah?

"Whiddon," Chester began.

But his friend cut him off. "No. Let me speak. I got an earful today, at the tavern. The whole village is awash with talk about her. They say she's angling for you, man. Some speculate that the whole reason she took the position with your grandmother was to get close to you."

All of the good cheer the evening had generated inside of her started to sour. Julia silently groaned.

"She's made you a target. And half of the village seems convinced you have fallen for it. Were you out with her last night? Someone spotted you, returning."

Each word was a blow and Julia's insides shriveled further as he talked. No. Not again. It was only a kiss. Or two. Why did scurrilous talk and sordid suspicions hound her?

But she rallied. Drew a long breath. She didn't have to fight alone this time. Chester might never be more than a friend, but he was that much, at least. He would defend her from such nasty gossip.

Breath caught, she waited.

Chester's tone, when he spoke, sounded soft. Gentle. Not filled with righteous indignation at all. "I want to thank you, Whiddon. I know you care for me, as I do for you. I know, without doubt, that you have my best interests at heart. Thank you for that."

Tears erupted. She bit back a sob as she backed away. Oh, she wished she hadn't eaten even the few bites. She felt sick. He wasn't going to defend her. How could he not, when he knew she despised baseless assumptions and being gossiped about in such a way? Hand over her mouth, she slipped out of the dining room and up the stairs.

Chester tamped down on his anger. "You are a brother to me. You always will be, my friend. That's why I hope you will listen now, Whiddon. Do not repeat what you have said. Indeed, forget that you have heard it. And as one of my most loyal friends, I expect that if you should hear such filth about Miss Deering again, you will knock the teeth out of the man spreading it."

"What? Wait! Where are you going?"

"To take care of this."

He let go of the cap on his anger as he stalked away. He might be glowing, he felt so incandescently angry. Searching through the guests, he could not find Julia. He did discover Mrs. Eckles in the parlor and asked if she'd spotted her.

"She went to the dining room to get a bite of supper."

"I must have missed her." He paused. His mind had been ticking away. He thought he knew who might be behind this injustice. "Mrs. Eckles, have you, by chance, seen Roland Graves in the house today?"

She looked startled. "Yes, sir. I believe he is in the kitchens now, visiting Ruby."

Chester didn't reply, he just flew across the house and down the stairs. Striding into the kitchen, he took stock. Mrs. Jensen was pouring a new bowl of wassail for Young Robert to take upstairs. Ruby stood near the cook's storage area, looking in. As he moved closer, Chester heard a crash and a cry come from inside.

He muscled Ruby aside. Charlie stood in the small space, glowering up at Roland Graves, a broken plate and crushed biscuits between them. Neither man nor boy noticed him.

"I already told you not to say anything against Miss Deering," Charlie hissed.

"And I told you, that light skirt is no better than she ought to be. You think I don't know your plan? To match that hussy with the earl? You are in cahoots with the wanton and I'm of a mind to tell him."

"We are neither of us any such thing!"

"She may think she's tangled Chester in her web, but that one is not the marrying type. He'll leave her ruined and cast aside and I'll see her run out of Farduff on a rail."

"*That is enough!*" Chester bellowed.

Ruby, Charlie and Graves all jumped.

Chester grabbed the man by his neckcloth and shoved him against a shelf.

Tears flowing, Charlie slipped past him and ran.

"Don't you *ever* say another word about or against Miss Deering," he growled.

"I know what I know," Graves squeaked. "Last night. You were seen—"

He shook the villain until his teeth clacked. "Do you think I didn't smell the smoke from your cheroots lingering in the corridor? I know what you saw—the two of us returning from laying the bonfire in the orchard. We meant it to be a surprise. And you are trying to turn it into something foul." He shook him again. "And as for what you are doing, lingering in my grandmother's house at all hours . . ." He glared over at Ruby, who flushed red.

Setting Graves down, Chester pushed him out into the kitchen, where he nearly fell over a chair. "You get out of this house. Now. And don't step foot in it again. If I hear another word spoken about Miss Deering in this village, I will come for you. You fancy yourself ill-used? Just wait until I hand you over to the press gangs that roam the London docks. A few years scrubbing decks and living on hard tack and grog will convince you otherwise."

Graves straightened and tried again. "I am a man of standing in this village—"

"Yes, and who owns the lease on the building that holds your shop? Who collects your rents?"

"Mr. Lincoln."

Chester laughed. "Yes. My grandmother's agent. You fool. Did you forget? Did you not know? How do you think she will react when she hears this? Is your petty campaign worth risking your family's living?"

Graves slumped. Without a glance at Ruby, he turned and left.

Chester turned a stern eye toward the kitchen maid. "I've heard no complaints about your service, Ruby, but if I discover that you've let that man back in this house, at any time, you will be dismissed."

The girl burst into tears and fled.

Chester closed his eyes for a moment, then went in search of Charlie.

CHAPTER 12

Julia pressed a cold cloth to her eyes. She couldn't stay in her room all night. Lady Chester needed her.

He doesn't owe you anything. So, the earl had kissed her. And she'd kissed him. That wasn't a promise of anything, even friendship. She took a deep breath. She would survive this. The dowager countess would help. All would be well, eventually.

Except for her broken heart.

She started as a loud knock sounded on her door. It swung open before she could respond, and the earl looked in.

She lifted her chin and stiffened her spine. She deserved at least the trappings of respect.

"Is Charlie in here with you?"

"No." The question startled her. "Why would you ask?"

"I can't find him. I've looked everywhere."

All of the starch went out of her. "What do you mean? He was enjoying the singing. And I saw him with a full plate of food. Has something happened?"

"Roland Graves has been besmirching your name. I found

Charlie confronting him. I put the fear of God into the weasel, but Charlie ran off."

Roland Graves spread the rumors? And Chester had put a stop to it? Had he defended her, after all? A weight dropped off her heart, but she gathered her scattered thoughts. Charlie was important now. "He must be here, somewhere." She had a sudden thought. "Did you ask his friend, Nick? He's been spending a lot of time with him."

"No. Come and help me find him?"

"Yes, of course."

Hurrying downstairs, they moved through the party. "Do you know which one is Nick?"

Chester looked at her. "You haven't met him?"

"No. Have you?"

"I've only seen him from a distance."

They didn't find anyone resembling his description, and no one had seen Charlie. When she began to ask about Nick, no one knew anything about him.

"He lives north of the village," she recalled. It didn't help. No one knew of such a man.

"Where could Charlie be?" Julia was starting to panic, now.

"Check the stables," Lady Chester ordered. "And the bonfire in the orchard."

"I've looked both places," Whiddon spoke up.

"Perhaps he left early for the midnight service at the church?" someone suggested.

They sent a group to look and to check the village. They organized another small group to go through the house. Chester checked the attics, but reported back, shaking his head.

Frowning, Julia wracked her brain and had a sudden thought. "You don't think he went out to the spot where we found the chestnuts?"

"So far? At night? In the cold?"

"You said he was angry?"

"Angry. Frightened. Perhaps . . . embarrassed." He nodded. "He just might go that far."

"I don't know where else to look," she despaired.

"I'll head out to investigate."

Julia looked helplessly at the dowager countess.

"Go on." Lady Chester waved at her. "I'm fine. The boy will respond to you. Find him and bring him home."

"Take my gig." Whiddon stepped forward. "It's fast."

"Thank you." A wealth of emotion sounded in Chester's voice as he gripped his friend's arm.

Julia said a few words to Mrs. Eckles, then ran to fetch her outer wear and a few blankets, too. She slipped out the back door and ran to the stables.

Chester and Whiddon turned to her. "We'll have to walk the last part," Chester said. "You can keep me on the right path."

They set out quickly. The sky was not as clear tonight, but the air was just as cold. Julia huddled into Chester's warmth. She prayed that Charlie, if he was out here, had bundled up warm enough.

They didn't speak at first. Julia leaned forward, as if her urgency could make the horse move faster. But guilt nagged at her. At last, she gathered her courage and tucked her arm beneath Chester's. "I owe you an apology."

He frowned down at her.

"I heard what Lord Whiddon said to you. What he heard at the Boar's Head. I heard you thank him for the news." Her breath hitched. "I ran. I thought you might believe what they were saying. I thought you weren't going to defend me." Casting her gaze down, she whispered, "I made a false assumption."

He blinked. "Well, damn." He watched the trail as he

absorbed her revelation. "You were right. False assumptions are *horrible*. They hurt like hell."

She laid her head on his shoulder. "I am so sorry."

"I shall forgive you," he said magnanimously. "Since you forgave me, mine."

"Thank you for taking care of Roland Graves."

"That weasel," he sniffed. Peering ahead, he began to pull back on the reins. "We walk from here."

He threw a blanket over the horse and she fetched one from the floor of the gig. Holding it close, she set out across the field and into the wood.

"We're nearly there," she said at last. She hurried toward the chestnut copse. "Oh! He's there!"

Charlie lay beneath the tree, eyes closed. He curled up against the cold, asleep. Nearby, the rabbit sat, chewing a cabbage leaf.

Julia reached over and clutched Chester's sleeve. "Is he—?"

He moved forward and the rabbit moved away. "He's fine. He's asleep. But he's cold. Bring the blanket."

Chester scooped the boy up and Charlie opened his eyes. He grimaced. "I'm sorry, sir."

"Sorry for what?" Chester asked roughly. "You faced that bounder down as if you were twice his size. You defended a lady." He gathered the boy into his arms and settled back, sitting with his back against the tree. "Good lad."

Charlie smiled groggily and let his head fall against Chester's shoulder. His eyes closed.

"Here." Julia offered the blanket.

"Wait. Open my coat for me, so I can tuck him up against me. Now the blanket." He looked up at her. "You get under here, too. I want to warm him up a bit before we start back."

She ducked under his arm and made sure they were all

covered. Kissing Charlie's head, she stretched her arms about them both.

With Chester's big, heated form under there, it soon grew warmer. Charlie's small body relaxed, and he slipped deeper into a more natural sleep. The quiet of the forest enfolded them. Though it was dark, moonlight lit the clouds, leaving an impression that another blanket wrapped them from above. Julia heard a small sound and looked up to see tears shining in Chester's eyes.

"I know what a family is," he said, low. "I know what it feels like, and how you miss it when it's gone. I had a happy childhood, you know. My father was wonderful. Big and strong. Loving. He made me laugh. He loved to laugh, and sing, and hunt, and eat. He loved to drink, too, I suspect." He chuckled.

Julia smiled. "He sounds lovely. My father rarely laughed. But he shared with me what he did love—books and learning and stories of the past. He loved me in his way. I never doubted it."

"Nor I. My father knew how to love. He adored my mother. She was . . . high strung. She liked to be the center of attention and resented anyone who stole her limelight. She often felt slighted or put upon, even by the smallest things. But my father could jolly her right out of a bad mood. He made her laugh, too, and focus elsewhere. They were happy, together." He sighed. "But then, he died."

"I'm sorry."

"We were devastated, of course. At first, I could scarcely imagine a world without my father in it. But my mother?" He shook his head. "Her grief and disbelief turned to bitterness. She railed at the unfairness of her loss. She raged at the world. We began to argue."

"Oh, no."

"She grew dourer and sourer with each day. She couldn't

tolerate any noise, any sign of life going on. Certainly, no laughter. A year after his death, she berated me for having fun with the village children. We quarreled all the time. At the end, she said such things." He swallowed. "I said them back, too. It was terrible. I set out for Grandmother's on my own. The servants thought it best, and they cooperated."

"And you set out to embrace life, to enjoy it, despite what she thought?"

"Hell, yes. I was loud and unruly every chance I got. I laughed. I sought out adventure, even scandal." He squeezed her hand where it rested on Charlie's leg. "I refused to look back or worry about anything behind me."

"Until I came along and bullied you into it," she said contritely. "No wonder you fought so hard."

"But you won, and I'm glad you did. Things were starting to careen out of control, to get frantic. I wanted to stop but didn't know how. Until you. You looked past the flurry and the flippancy and you saw me."

"Just as you saw me," she whispered.

"You made me slow down, breathe, and at last, I could think again. Feel again. I'm not sure I'll ever reconcile with my mother, but I feel myself again, as if I've started over." He raised his chin and pointed with it. "Look around us. Look where we are." He smiled down at Charlie. "I've begun again, a new life, filled with vast wonders and possibilities—but Julia?"

She raised her eyes to his.

"I need you to agree to share it with me. It's all for naught, if you are not by my side."

Now she blinked back tears.

"Will you? Will you come and live with me, laugh with me, and be my love?"

She grinned. "Try and stop me."

He laughed.

"I never thought to find love," she confessed. "I thought it was not for me. And then you toppled over onto your back before me." She laughed up at him. "Your massive shoulders bewitched me, but it was your caring that undid me. No one ever looked past the oddities to see the girl inside, until you." Her mouth twitched. "And then you kissed her."

"Ah, well, that explains it," he said with a grin. "Move up a little, so I can do it again."

They had to stretch and strain, but they managed to get close enough to kiss, sealing a thousand promises with the press of their lips.

Their struggle, however, awakened Charlie. He opened his eyes and peered up at them.

"Finally," he said with a grin.

EPILOGUE

The hour was later than originally intended the next morning, Christmas Morning, when they all gathered, after a hearty breakfast, to exchange gifts.

"Where's Whiddon?" Grandmama asked.

"He has gone," Chester told her. His friend had spent a few minutes with Julia before he left. He didn't know what was said, but he knew Whiddon had done the right thing. He knew it hadn't been easy, and that his friend was troubled by all that had happened to their group over the last year. He made a note to check on him, soon.

For right now, though, there were gifts. He didn't need anything, himself. He smiled across at Julia. He'd received the gift that would eclipse all others, forever.

Standing, he rubbed his hands together. "We were betrothed just in the nick of time. Now it is entirely appropriate for me to give you a gift at Christmas." He presented her with a basket.

"How lovely." She explored the wealth of lavender scented lotions, sachets and ointments.

"They are made by a group of women sponsored by Lady Hope Tensford. She is a friend, and I can't wait for you to meet her." He smiled just thinking of it. "I want you to know all of my friends, as soon as possible."

"I cannot wait either," she said with a smile.

"As for you," he said to his grandmother. He waggled his brows at her and brought out a heavy box to lay at her feet.

"Well, go on. Open it for me," she ordered.

He did and lifted out the first of a set of luxuriously bound books. "*The Lattimere Legends*. I know you prize your first editions, but I thought you might enjoy a fancy set, as well."

His grandmother rubbed a gnarled finger over the soft leather before she looked up at him and cackled with laughter. "Oh, you dear boy. You couldn't have chosen better." Reaching for another volume, she held them in her lap. "I might as well tell you, now."

"Tell us what?" asked Julia.

"About my theatrical piece for tonight."

"You are reading from the *Legends*, are you not?"

"I am." She looked around at them all. "I am also claiming my authorship of them."

Chester grinned. "I had my suspicions."

"Well, I did not!" Julia leaned over and gripped Grandmama's arm. "How lovely. And how clever you are."

"I should have done it long ago. I didn't because I was afraid it would reflect badly upon my Chester, or perhaps our children. Later, I just didn't want to face the furor. But it's time. I want to own my hard work. I'm tired of that pasty son of Lord Carnham's smiling coyly when he's asked if he wrote them. I am a woman of strength and ability and it's time the world knew it."

"Well said," Julia agreed.

His grandmother met his gaze directly. "As you are facing your demons, my boy, how could I do any less?"

Leaning over, he kissed her hand.

"Now," his grandmother said brusquely. "It is your turn. Julia, do you have it ready?"

"I do." His betrothed went and took something from beneath the sideboard. Smiling, she came over and indicated that he should sit on the settee, then she set it in his lap.

It was a wooden box, stained dark and attractively carved.

"Open it and you'll see that it is from the both of us," his grandmother ordered.

"I do see." The lid underneath was padded and lined with a lovely piece of embroidery. He blinked rapidly as he touched the dear face peering through the window. She'd put her heart into this. "I don't know how, but you captured Ensign completely." He looked between them both. "Thank you."

"Open the pouch," Grandmama gestured.

The velvet pouch felt light.

"Now, that is for both of you," his grandmother said. "I meant to give you your grandfather's pocket watch, but today I feel that this is more appropriate."

He spilled the contents out. "Oh," he breathed. "I had forgotten."

It was a lovely bracelet, made of gemstones and wire and glass to resemble the green leaves and white berries of mistletoe. "I remember you wearing it, when Grandfather lived."

"I couldn't bear to wear it after he'd gone, but now Julia must wear it."

He turned to his betrothed and took her wrist. Fastening the bracelet over her wrist, he smiled at the wonder in her face.

"You wear it at Christmas, and you are never without mistletoe," he told her. Happy to demonstrate, he raised her hand over her head. She smiled in comprehension and he leaned in to kiss her softly.

A knock sounded on the front door. Charlie leapt to his feet. "It's Nick! It must be!" The boy ran out and Chester and the women all exchanged surprised looks.

"He did it!" Charlie came back, carrying a box. "I asked for his help and he did it." He laid the box at Julia's feet.

"Please ask Charlie's friend to join us," Grandmama said to Young Robert, who came to the doorway.

"The gentleman said he could not tarry, but he sends you best wishes for the season."

Chester stood to peer out the window. He saw the same portly silhouette he'd glimpsed before, moving down the lane towards the street. As he watched, the man turned and gave him a nod and a salute.

"I was afraid you might be lonely when we left," Charlie was telling Julia. "I knew you couldn't bring your wild friend here."

"You are very thoughtful, Charlie." Julia smiled at the boy.

"Open it," Charlie ordered.

She did and exclaimed to find a tiny rabbit inside, with an adorably pink nose and black fur.

"This one is young. Nick says he can learn to live in the house, just like a cat. He's an orphan too, like me. He can be your friend when I am gone."

Tears showed in her eyes. "I would love to make him my friend, Charlie, and I hope you will help."

"Yes, I'll do all I can, before we go."

"That's the thing." Chester looked over at Julia as he squatted down before the boy. She nodded and he met Charlie's gaze. "Miss Deering has agreed to marry, me, Charlie.

We would like you to stay with us, afterwards. If you wish to, of course."

"Stay with you? Live with you? Like a family?"

"Exactly like that."

The boy made a strangled sound and Chester caught him as he leaped into his arms. "Yes. Please."

They all needed a moment with their handkerchiefs after that.

"There is a small problem," Chester said, eventually.

"What is it?" Charlie spoke into his chest.

"We will have to be careful and be sure that Julia's new friend gets along with your new friend."

The boy straightened. "My new friend?"

Young Robert was at the door again. He knelt down and set a wriggling mastiff puppy on the floor. Charlie gave a half sob, half laugh and the pup's ears perked. They met in the middle of the room, in a riot of laughter, tears, wiggling tail and short, happy barks.

"Another case of love at first sight," Chester said with a sigh, taking Julia's hand.

Eventually, order was restored. The rest of the gifts were exchanged. Charlie loved the illustrated book of legends about King Arthur that Julia had for him. Chester praised the riding gloves from his grandmother. He whispered a promise about a betrothal ring to come in Julia's ear.

They all settled, quietly, at last. Peace descended. Tired, young animals dropped off to sleep in arms.

"Goodness," Julia said as she leaned against him and stroked long, silky ears in her lap. "We must go and get ready for the theatrical."

"First, a toast." He rose and went to the sideboard and poured wine for them all, just a little watered down for Charlie. "And in case you had any doubt that this is a momentous day, you may see that Mrs. Eckles has dug out the whole set of the king's goblets." He passed them around.

"To slowing down," Julia said, raising her cup at him.

"To starry nights," he replied softly.

"To family," Charlie said.

"To the magic of Christmas," Grandmama declared.

And they all drank to that.

ABOUT THE AUTHOR

USA Today Bestselling author Deb Marlowe adores History, England and Men in Boots. Clearly she was destined to write Historical Romance.

A Golden Heart winner and Rita nominee, Deb writes Regency Romance and Young Adult Fantasy Adventure.

A proud geek, history buff and story addict, she loves to talk with readers! Find her discussing books, movies, TV, recipes from Deb Marlowe's Regency Kitchen and her infamous Men in Boots on Facebook, Twitter, Instagram, and Pinterest.

Connect with Deb
www.DebMarlowe.com
Deb@DebMarlowe.com

Lady Tamsyn and the Pixie's Curse

Lord Locryn and the Pixie's Kiss

and coming soon:

Miss Penneck and the Pixie's Poem

Writing as D.M. Marlowe:

The Eye of the Ninja Chronicles

Eye of the Ninja

Obsidian's Eye

The Fire in the Ice